THE INN AT PELICAN BEACH

PELICAN BEACH SERIES BOOK ONE

MICHELE GILCREST

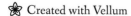

PAYTON

$\mathcal{I}$ leaned over the balcony staring at the ocean while longing to wash my sorrows away. The sound of the crashing waves was like medicine to my shattered soul. At forty-two, with no children, and a finalized divorce, I was left alone to pick up the pieces. My ex-husband, Jack, was off indulging in his new life as a bachelor. For now, at least. The divorce papers didn't seem to impact him much whenever he missed me and wanted to come home. This time I was fed up. My parents needed help with the family business at the Inn. The Pelican Beach area was an upscale community with all of the relaxing pleasantries of living near the water. Whenever the summer season rolled around, the beach clubs and rentals were booked to maximum capacity. Moving back home was just what I needed to heal old wounds and get a fresh start.

"Aunt Payton, can I have some candy?"

I was startled, not realizing that my niece was standing right behind me.

"Maggie, Sweetie, let's check with mom first. I think it's almost time for dinner."

"Okay, but I bet mom won't care if you say yes."

"I'm not falling for your tricks, little one."

I bent over and gently grabbed Maggie's cheeks and kissed her.

"You almost got me in trouble the last time we were together. Come on. Let's go inside and see what Gram is preparing for dinner."

She slid the glass doors open and joined everyone in the family room.

My parents' cottage home was like a picture-perfect getaway. The recent renovations brightened the walls with white shiplap, low hanging fans, and wooden beams on the ceiling. The sheer curtains blew in the wind, and the beach themed decor made it all the more inviting.

"Abby, you might want to keep an extra eye on your daughter." I took the opportunity to playfully snitch on my niece when we went inside.

"Uh, oh."

Abby glanced at Maggie and gave her a look of disapproval while standing with her hands on her hips.

"What did she do now?"

"Nothing yet. She's warming up, though. I'd keep an eye on her."

Maggie knew her Mom wasn't really upset with her. She lowered her head and looked up in slight amusement.

"Maggie, go with your brother and get washed up for dinner."

With the mannerisms of an angel, she replied, "Yes, Ma'am."

We all knew to watch that little smile.

The kids ran off, challenging one another to see who could get to the bathroom first. I watched as my sister Abby turned and gave my outfit the once over.

"Payton, you look like you need a little sisterly TLC."

I looked down at myself, observing a slightly disheveled but totally comfortable jogging suit.

"Why? Is something wrong with my outfit?"

"Your outfit, your hair, your..."

"Okay, okay. I get it. Look. I'm fine. Besides, we're just hanging around the house. I'm not trying to impress anybody."

"No fooling."

It's not that I didn't care about my appearance altogether. At about 5'5 weighing one hundred twenty pounds, I think I carried myself rather well. I usually kept my hair in a ponytail or a bun. Sometimes I wore it out. If I'm heading out, I throw on some yoga pants and my signature lipgloss. It was still a feminine look, in my opinion.

"I have an idea. Let's give each other make-overs later on after dinner."

I rolled my eyes and let out a deep sigh that sounded like hissing through my teeth.

"Oh, Payton. It will be so much fun. Pleassse?"

I tried shifting my attention to the big television screen above the mantle.

"Seriously, Sis. The last thing we want you to do is to come back home and mope around. It will be so uplifting."

"Mmm, hmm."

"Come on. Mom is excited to have all of us together again. Even your wicked sister Becca is going to take time out of her busy schedule to be here this weekend. You know she's going to walk in here looking like something straight out of a magazine."

"Are you two still at odds?"

"Oh no, not us. We're peachy."

"I know what that means."

"You know your sister."

"I know both of my sisters!"

"Well, whenever all three of Mom's girls get together, it's worth sprucing up a little bit. Don't you think?"

"Abby, surely you have something better to do?"

"I'll quit if you say yes."

Begrudgingly I gave in. "Alright already. Let's just move it to Friday night. I have to be up bright and early to help at the Inn tomorrow."

"Deal!"

Just then, our mother, Helen, walked into the room.

"What kind of deal are we making?"

"Payton agreed to get a make-over by yours truly."

"Abby! Your sister hasn't been back for two minutes, and you're already trying to fix her up. Some things haven't changed since you two were little."

"Mom has a point, Abby. You always used to torture me like a doll when we were kids."

"Oh, stop it. I always made you look glamorous, and you know it," she teased.

"Glamorous?" I flipped my hair back and modeled across the room to mock Abby's description of the experience. Somehow we managed to see it differently.

Mom took great delight in having us together again.

"Look at you two having fun just like old times. I love it. Just wait until your father gets home. He's going to be just as happy as I am."

"I love it too," Abby agreed. "I'm glad you're back, Sis. I'll have to find reasons to make my way over here every week just to pluck your nerves."

"Thanks, Ab. Looking forward to it. Hey, how is my brother-in-law these days?"

"He's better than ever. At the top of his A-game as he would say."

"Is he joining us for dinner?"

4

"He can't make it tonight, he's working late. The firm is preparing for a huge trial. You know how that is."

"Sounds like a lot of long, sleepless nights."

"Exactly."

I hesitated before responding. "Well, I know Wyatt's a good man. Just make sure he doesn't get in the habit of having too many long, sleepless nights."

"Payton Matthews, watch your tongue. Your sister's marriage has absolutely nothing to do with what you went through."

I immediately felt guilty and shifted my tone.

"You're right. Sorry, Abby."

"No need to apologize. I know you didn't mean any harm by it."

"I just don't understand it." I walked toward the kitchen counter to begin helping with dinner prep.

"I thought I was doing all the right things as a wife. I had all of his meals ready after a long day, I cleaned the house, and did everything I could to create a loving home. It seemed like all I received in return were late nights and more and more time apart."

I tried to fight back the tears.

"It's going to be okay, Sis. It may not seem like it right now, but you are going to heal from this and be stronger than ever."

"She's right, Payton. You'll get through this."

Our conversation was interrupted by the sound of glass shattering on the floor. Everybody chimed in unison.

"The kids!"

Abby left the kitchen heading in one direction while simultaneously, the doorbell rang.

"Good grief. Shut the oven off for me, Payton. I'm going to see who's at the door."

No sooner than I turned off the oven and patted my face dry, my niece ran into the kitchen.

"Aunt Payton, where's Gram?"

"She went to answer the front door, Maggie. Is everything okay?"

"Aidan knocked her flowers on the floor. It was an accident. Now he's crying cause he thinks Gram will be upset."

"Oh, I'm sure Gram won't be upset. We just have to teach him to be careful, that's all."

Abby returned to the kitchen to get a broom.

"Maggie, you have to set a good example for Aidan. Next time tell him no running around the house. Okay?"

"Yes, Mama."

Mom returned to the kitchen, looking like a nervous wreck. "Payton, do you have a second?"

"Sure."

She motioned for me to step out in the hall.

"Jack is at the front door."

"Are you kidding me?"

"I wish. I can send him away if you want me to," Mom said.

"Unbelievable. I'll take care of it."

I walked to the front door but didn't say a word as Jack stood on the other side of the threshold.

"Hi, Payton."

I looked at him but didn't speak.

"I was hoping I could talk to you."

"There's nothing to talk about, Jack. We're divorced now, remember? I signed the papers that you served weeks ago. Case closed."

"I know. I was foolish. That's why I'm here to apologize and to try and make things right."

I looked at him as if he had lost his mind.

"Let me get this straight. You were living this whole other

life outside of our marriage, but I forgave you. Then you did it again and had the nerve to serve me with divorce papers. Now you want to make things right?"

"I know it looks bad."

"Oh, it's bad! So bad you don't know if you're coming or going. You can't tell up from down or left from right. But I'll tell you one thing I'm very clear about. It's over between us, Jack!"

Slamming the door felt good before re-opening to leave one last impression.

"Do yourself a favor and don't come back here again. Leave me and my family alone!"

The final slam was empowering. This was just what I needed to propel me into the next chapter of my life.

PAYTON

*M*y first day back at the Inn began in guest services greeting the arriving guests.

"Good morning, Welcome to the Inn at Pelican Beach."

"Thank you. This place is gorgeous."

"Is this your first time visiting the Inn?"

"Yes, we're on our honeymoon."

"That's wonderful. Congratulations."

"Thank you."

One couldn't help but notice how happy and in love they appeared to be. I remember those days just like it was yesterday.

"I'm sure you're excited to get settled in. My name is Payton. I'll go over a few of our services with you and get you all checked in."

"Sounds good."

"May I have your name?"

"Jonathan and Samantha Mitchell. Here's our I.D."

"Great. It looks like you booked the Ocean Breeze Suite. A lovely choice for our newlyweds. You'll have a private balcony where you can enjoy an early sunrise breakfast or a beautiful sunset dinner. If you want concierge service, all you have to do is dial zero, and they'll be happy to assist. Beach towels will be provided in your room. Do you have any questions for me?"

The gentleman looked at his wife and then answered.

"No, I think we're all set."

"Wonderful. Here are your keys. Enjoy your stay."

My father, William Matthews, had a way of being a prankster at times. He snuck up on me from behind.

"You still have the magic touch. It's like you never left."

"Aw, Dad. You're a little biased, don't you think?"

"Maybe, but you're good, Payton. Honestly, your return couldn't have come at a better time."

"Thanks, Dad. Just let me know whatever you need. If I can recall correctly, I was the jack of all trades the last time I worked here with you and mom. Room inventory, bookings, dining services. You name it."

"We did have you all over the place, didn't we?"

"You sure did."

"Well, we can chat more later. I have a few ideas in mind about how you can be of help to us. Maybe we can have some father-daughter time later and talk things over?"

"Of course."

"Great. In the meantime, I have a ten o'clock meeting with a gentleman by the name of Cole Miller. I asked him to stop by the front desk. If you wouldn't mind sending him my way, that would be great."

"No problem."

"Thanks, Honey. I'll see you in a little bit."

He started to walk away before turning around with a final thought.

"Payton."

"Yes, Dad?"

"Make sure you talk to your mother about creating a flexible schedule. I don't want you two in here fifteen plus hours every day like me. Get out to the beach and get some sun."

"But..."

"No buts. What good is the Inn to the family if we're not healthy enough to enjoy the fruits of our labor? It's time to start taking care of you. Daddy's orders."

"Aye aye, Captain."

I raised my hands and saluted my father before making my way back to the front desk. I couldn't argue with him if I tried. He always had the heart to take good care of his girls. Besides, the view of the water and the warm breeze made it very tempting to give in to his request.

A lady approached the desk dressed in housekeeping attire.

"Good morning. You must be Miss Matthews."

"Yes, I am. And you are..."

"I'm Shelby." Shelby extended her hand to greet me with a smile that instantly warmed my heart.

"I work for your parents here at the Inn. I'm on the house-keeping team."

"Oh, it's so nice to meet you."

"Thank you, and welcome back. Your parents talk about you all the time. It's nice to finally meet you."

While Shelby spoke, I noticed her glossing over my outfit. I guess I really needed to get my act together in the clothing department.

"You and Mrs. Matthews look very much alike."

I leaned over and whispered, "Shh, don't tell anybody I'm wearing my mother's clothes. I promise not to make it a habit."

Shelby laughed hard and tried to quickly regain her composure.

"You're funny."

"It's our little secret. You can just keep it between us."

I tapped my fingers on my lips to further emphasize the secret part. Mainly I was just making light of it. My family knows how much I couldn't care less about clothing.

"Your secret is safe with me, Miss Matthews."

"Oh, please call me Payton."

"Payton it is. Again, it's so nice to meet you. I have to begin my shift, but I'm sure we'll see each other soon."

"Have a great day."

"You too." Shelby had such a sweet demeanor about her. It made me grateful that my parents placed a lot of emphasis on carefully choosing the staff.

For the sake of not embarrassing the family, I made clothes shopping an item on my to-do list. This morning I settled for borrowing a few pieces out of my mother's closet to make it through, but it couldn't be a permanent plan. My former days were spent in yoga pants unless I was going to a photoshoot. Even then, my attire was much more relaxed. My father's style was business casual. He always wore Khakis, loafers, and white collared shirts. Perhaps even a golf shirt toward the end of the week. Mom, on the other hand, was classy at all times. She loved neutral colors and was always laced with pearls.

I continued jotting down my plans for the day when I noticed a tall man approaching the front desk. His light blue eyes instantly caught my attention.

"Welcome to the Inn at Pelican Beach."

"Why, thank you. My name is Cole Miller. I have a ten o'clock appointment with Mr. Matthews."

"Yes, he's expecting you. I'll dial his extension to let him know you're here."

While I dialed my father's extension, I watched Mr. Miller as he looked around and began taking measurements.

"Dad, Mr. Miller is here."

"Okay, send him down to my office."

"Sure thing."

I stepped from behind the desk to get his attention. He was so busy scoping out the place I just stood there and waited for him to look my way.

"I'm sorry, I didn't realize you were off the phone."

"Yes, I thought I'd come over to see what you were doing."

"Oh, I was just looking around. I'm here to talk about a few renovation plans with Mr. Matthews."

"That explains the measuring tape."

"Yep, I never leave home without it."

I nodded and then extended my hand to direct him down the hall.

"He's waiting for you in his office. Second door to your right."

"Thank you, Miss..."

"Payton," I responded.

"Miss Payton."

"Just Payton."

I waited for him to walk away before returning to the desk.

"Strange."

My mother appeared from the back office just in time to hear my comment.

"There's nothing strange about Cole Miller. He has one of the most talented renovation teams in town."

"Were you eavesdropping on me?"

"No, you were talking out loud to yourself."

"Right."

"Cole completed the renovations for the cottage."

"Impressive."

"Exactly. He's very talented. He has a lovely beach house not far from here where he and his daughter, Emmie, live. I think his mother spends a lot of time helping to take care of her when he's working."

"Where's his wife?"

"She died from cancer about five or six years ago."

"That's so sad."

"Isn't it?"

"You know, Mom, the area hasn't changed much since I left. It's still a quaint little town in Florida where everyone knows each other by name. Yet we attract so many new visitors as well."

"Therein lies the beauty. That's what makes the Pelican Beach area so special. You have the small mom and pop businesses, neighbors who've known each other for decades, the water, boat life. This is what you call home."

"To us, maybe, but to our guests, this is what you call a vacation. We need to get back to work."

"Speaking of work. You know your father wants to have a talk with you about where you'd like to fit in here at the Inn. He told me he had a few ideas. He's so excited that you're home."

"He mentioned something in passing this morning. I'm excited to be back. I know I promised I would help run the Inn until I get back on my feet."

"I feel a but coming on."

"Not really. I just don't want you guys to think that I plan to stay underneath you at the house or here for an indefinite amount of time."

"Sweetheart, we don't think that at all. Even though I hope you know if you wanted to, you could."

"I knew you would say that, but I don't want to take advantage. At some point, I'll have to learn how to get back out there and stand on my own two feet. There's nothing wrong with me getting my own place, supporting myself, and pursuing my dreams again."

"Are you talking about your freelance photography?"

"Yes. I want to help out at the Inn, and during my spare time, I also want to start re-establishing a list of clients."

"I think that's a wonderful idea. I'm sure your father will be supportive. Just tell him."

"I will, but I didn't want to disappoint him if he has his heart set on something else."

"He'll be fine. I'm sure he'd much rather see you happy."

"Thanks."

"How are you feeling after last night's shenanigans with Jack?"

"I'm fine. It's not like he hasn't pulled a stunt like that before. I just think that following me out to your house was taking things a bit far. He made his bed, now it's time for him to lay in it."

"I'm not worried about him at all. As long as you understand how valuable you are and how this wasn't your fault."

"I know."

"Okay. I'm going to put the topic to rest and go to work on the schedule. And yes, I already know your father wants us to keep the schedule flexible. Take care of yourself first and bla bla bla."

"What's going on with you two? Dad just gave me a whole speech this morning about this very topic."

"I don't know what his problem is, but he's been harping on me about my work ethic long before you arrived. Apparently, I work too many hours and need to take time off. I don't pay him any mind. He forgets that it took the two of us to build this place from the ground up."

"Well, there must be something to it, Mom."

"I guess. By the way, Nancy, who normally works at the front desk, will be here in the next hour. After she gets here, make sure you go to the kitchen and grab yourself a bite to eat. Chef's crab cakes are to die for!"

"I was thinking of using my lunch break to visit a clothing store or two. I need some new clothes in the worst way."

"That's not a bad idea. Eat lunch, and then go. We'll be here when you get back."

She disappeared back to her office, which was down a separate hall from Dad's. With a little downtime, I decided to open my journal and list a few locations I wanted to photograph. In my spare time, I thought it might be a great idea to work on a website that would be used to display some of my best photography work.

"Grove Point Lighthouse, Main Street boardwalk, Pelican Cliffs."

The list would have to wait. I could hear my father escorting Cole back to the front lobby. I set my journal aside to greet them.

"So, what do you think, Cole?"

Cole took a minute to gather his thoughts before responding.

"I think the project and the time frame is doable. Let me take a look at the numbers and get back to you by the beginning of next week."

"I'm looking forward to it."

The gentlemen shook hands and parted ways. Cole walked past the front desk and tipped his hat toward me. "Have a good day."

"You too."

I added a few more ideas to my list before stopping to make a phone call. On the other end of the line, I heard my father talking and started to hang up. I realized that I had accidentally hit my father's extension and attempted to gently place the phone down. I confess that overhearing what appeared to be a tense conversation caused me to reconsider hanging up.

"William, we may be new to working together, but I'm not

new to crunching numbers. I can confidently say that your numbers are not adding up. As your accountant, I'm advising you that you're about to enter the danger zone if you don't stop all of the frivolous spending."

"I keep my own records, and everything is balanced. What on earth are you talking about?"

"My records show quite the opposite. You need to come in and go through this with me before you find yourself in so deep you can't get out."

"You've got to be kidding me. I don't have any time for this. We're about to start some renovations at the Inn to help attract more business."

"William, renovating is the last thing that should be on your mind right now. Do you want to lose the Inn?"

"Of course not."

"Well, your lenders are certain to start sending threats at the rate you're going. You need to come down here to straighten this mess out, or that's exactly what will happen."

There was an abrupt end to the telephone call with nothing but silence on the other end of the line. I hung up and was frozen in disbelief. My dad had always been good at handling the finances. There had to be some sort of mistake.

PAYTON

O n Saturday morning, my sisters and I gathered around Mom's table before heading down to the beach.

"The last one down to the beach is a rotten egg." Abby and I weren't the least bit enthused.

My youngest sister, Rebecca, was an attractive thirty-year-old, with a successful career and a very competitive spirit. She was pretty much spoiled rotten from birth and had a particular way of getting underneath Abby's skin. We used to always argue because it seemed like Rebecca continuously got away with murder. As an adult, she had a way with men and still does if you ask me. They all swoon over her hourglass shape and bouncy, long blond curls. She had them lined up for days to spend time with her, but it never seemed to develop into anything serious.

"Some things never change. You two are still no fun."

"Don't start, Becca. This is not a competition." Abby snapped at Rebecca as if they were right back in high school.

As always, I had to play the role of a mediator. "Quit you

two. We just got together, and you're already starting trouble. Can we enjoy ourselves, please?"

"Yes," Abby answered. Then she stared over at Rebecca, who didn't say anything.

"Why do I always have to be the voice of reason with you two? If anything, I'm the one who needs help right now. Not the other way around."

"You're right, Sis." Rebecca held my arm as we walked along the sand to find the perfect spot.

"How are you doing?"

"I can think of better times in my life, but I'm trying not to dwell on the bad. Something positive that's come from all this is being back home in Pelican Beach."

"Plus, she has this stunning new make-over to kick off her new beginnings." Abby fluffed my hair in the back. "Your hair does look gorgeous, Payton."

"Thanks, Becca. So tell us what's been going on in your world?"

"The usual. My head is buried in the sand of criminal cases with barely any time to come up for air. Occasionally I run into our brother in law down at the court." Rebecca looked over at Abby while referring to her husband, Wyatt.

"He's getting to be a big-time hot shot lawyer from what I'm hearing around town. Congratulations, Abby."

"Thanks, I guess."

We paused to pick out a spot to lay our towels and picnic baskets.

"You guess? Aren't you happy? I wish I had the luxury of having a husband who was bringing in the big bucks. That way, I could put the kids on the school bus and try to decide between a tennis match or a mani-pedi for the day."

Rebecca rubbed sunscreen all over her body and proceeded to act nonchalant about what she just said.

"Rebecca, that's low. You have no idea what my life is like. I'm not quite sure why you're always trying to take a stab at me outside of being jealous."

"Jealous?"

Again I had to interrupt the charade. This was starting to get old.

"Enough. For crying out loud. If you start with each other one more time, I'm going back inside."

"Well, then tell your little sister over there to stop acting so childish."

"Abby!" I scolded her just like a little child.

Abby held up her hands in surrender and then returned to spreading out her towel.

"Seriously, you two. We have a much bigger problem on our hands that we need to discuss."

Finally, I had their attention as they looked at me with concern.

"Abby, I didn't have a chance to say anything yesterday because mom was around. I figured today would be better so we could all talk."

"What is it?"

"I overheard dad having a disturbing conversation about the finances for the Inn yesterday. He was talking to the accountant, but it didn't sound good."

Rebecca dismissively waved her hand over my comment. "Those two are always going at it. That's nothing new."

"Really?" I was confused as to why Rebecca hadn't mentioned anything about it.

"You knew about this?"

"I know there's been plenty of times that I drop by and dad's grouchy over one thing or another having to do with money. Mom always seems to think he has everything under control, so I stay out of it."

"Okay, well, what I heard didn't sound like everything is under control. The accountant was basically telling Dad if he didn't get his act together, he could lose the Inn."

"That can't be good," Abby said.

"Exactly. Meanwhile, Dad had just finished meeting with Cole Miller with intentions of starting renovations at the Inn soon. I don't get it. It doesn't make sense. If they're having money problems, the last thing they need is to spend more money."

Abby had a look of concern on her face. "I feel terrible. I didn't have a clue any of this was going on. I stop by the Inn every once in a while, but I've been so busy with the kids I just assumed all was well."

"Wouldn't it be better for us to confirm if it's true first?" Rebecca was the only one that didn't seem to buy into what I was saying.

Before waiting for a response, she added, "The Matthews men and women are a strong bunch who won't settle without a fight. If the business is really in trouble, we'll all rally together and do something about it."

"Fair enough. So who's going to be the one to bring it up to Dad?"

"Not me. I wasn't there to overhear the conversation." Becca was quick to take herself out of the mix, and as usual, Abby didn't miss an opportunity to jump on her case.

"What happened to all of the big and bad talk about how strong we are?"

I shook my head in disgust.

"Forget it. I'll say something at the appropriate time. Dad's been saying he wants to talk about my role at the Inn. Maybe that will be the appropriate time for me to gently bring it up."

"It's probably best since you were there to hear the conver-

-

sation anyway. If we were to all say something, it would probably make Dad uncomfortable."

"Abby does have a good point, Payton."

I agreed and decided to wait for the right time to talk to him.

PAYTON

"*P*ayton, I'd like you to officially meet Cole Miller."

Mom was grinning like a Cheshire cat.

"Ah, yes, we met last week when Cole was here to talk to Dad."

"I didn't know you two are related. Mrs. Matthews, I see good genes run in the family."

"Oh, Cole. You sure know how to stay on my good side." Mom was tickled pink by every word that came out of his mouth.

"Payton, I was hoping you could work with Cole on the renovation project for the Inn. You know, be there in case he has questions or needs anything."

"Sure. I didn't realize the project was starting so soon. I thought Dad was waiting to hear back on the numbers."

Cole offered more information to clarify.

"Your father and I spoke toward the end of the weekend. I shared the numbers with him, and he said everything was a go."

"Alright. Well, Dad knows best."

Mom looked as if she was enjoying the idea of us working

together. In my opinion, she was up to something. Something I probably wouldn't approve of.

"Wonderful. So I guess we need the two of you to sit down and coordinate dates and a few logistics for the front lobby. I'm certain the end result will be magnificent; however, in no way should it hinder our guests from entering in and out of the Inn."

"Don't worry, Ma'am. We have you covered. The team will create a temporary entrance and will be sure to stay out of everyone's way."

"Lovely. I trust you, Cole. You did an excellent job at the house, and I know you'll do it again."

"Yes, Ma'am."

"Payton, would you like to take Cole to the conference room?"

"Sure."

"Your father and I were thinking that it might be a wonderful space for you to work until we establish a more suitable office."

"The conference room is perfect. Cole, if you're ready, you can follow me."

I grabbed my memo pad and laptop on my way to the back. I felt a little nervous. Perhaps even a bit rusty. Nevertheless, I didn't want to disappoint, so I decided to fake it until I made it.

"Please have a seat."

"Thank you."

"Before we get started, can I offer you a bottle of water?"

"No, thank you. I'm pretty good."

Cole made his way to the other side of the table. Standing almost six feet tall, he easily towered over me. However, the warmth from his smile reduced any amount of intimidation when talking to him. Cole had a laid back presence about him. His business attire consisted of Khaki shorts, a polo shirt, and boat shoes. I guess it was the nature of his business that allowed him to be so casual.

"Okay, I'm just going to pull up our calendar to make sure we're on the same page with the dates. While I wait for it to load, why don't we begin with your plans to create a separate entrance for the guests."

"Certainly. I'm just going to have my crew section off one half of the front lobby at a time. We'll use dividers so everyone can still have easy access to wherever they need to go."

"That sounds good. I would imagine your crew will have a cut off time as not to disturb the guests during dinner hours?"

"Absolutely. The crew will finish up promptly at five o'clock. We'll have a divider up so you will never have to worry about there being an interference with materials lying around or the guys getting in the way."

"Perfect. The notes on the calendar say that I need to block off two weeks. Can I pencil you in for..."

"Thursday."

"Wow, okay. You don't waste any time. Thursday it is. That means the project should be all wrapped up before July 1st?"

"It looks that way."

"That's exciting. Well, everything is all set on the calendar. The only other thing I want to confirm is the financial piece. Has my father already made arrangements with you, or do I need to check in with him?"

"We're all set with the finances. He cut a check for the first half of the project, so we should be good to go."

I gulped as I tried to digest what he was saying. How in the world did my father manage to write a check knowing that he still faced some unanswered questions with his accountant? I had a feeling in the pit of my stomach that was uneasy, but I just had to trust that he knew what he was doing.

"Is everything okay?"

I got a little uncomfortable and shifted in my chair.

"Yes, I'm sorry. I think we're good. If you have any questions or your crew members need anything feel free to call me."

"Great." Cole stood up and extended his hand across the table. He had a confident grip that was sure to leave a lasting impression. We exited the meeting room and made our way back to the front lobby.

"How long have you been here?" Cole asked.

"Pardon me?"

"In Pelican Beach. I don't recall seeing you around before now."

"Oh, I just returned last week."

"Last week? Wow, you didn't waste any time getting to work."

"You're right about that. When I told Mom and Dad I was moving back, they said they could use some help at the Inn, so here I am."

"When I saw you the other day, I had no idea I was talking to the boss' daughter."

"Yep, that's me. I'm one of the boss' daughters, I should say. There are three of us."

"Did you and your husband buy a place out here or..."

"No. I'm staying with my folks for a little while until I get settled and decide where I want to live. I'm divorced."

"I'm sorry."

We stopped at the front desk, where Rebecca walked in and placed her expensive bag on the counter.

"Perfect timing, Sis. I stopped by to see if you wanted to have the money talk with Dad."

I stared at Rebecca, silently pleading with her to shut up in front of Cole.

"Oh. Excuse me. How could I miss such a handsome man

standing right here in front of me? My name is Rebecca Matthews, and you are?"

"Cole Miller, nice to meet you." Cole started blushing.

It was all I could do to keep from rolling my eyes. I couldn't stand it when Rebecca was so forward with men.

Cole shook her hand.

"Ladies, I'm going to let you catch up. I have an appointment that I need to get to. Payton, I'll see you bright and early on Thursday morning. Rebecca, it was nice meeting you."

"Have a great dayyyy."

"You too."

Rebecca watched him as he walked out of the Inn.

"Good Lord, that man is hot."

I stood, staring at Rebecca as she watched Cole leave.

"What? It's not my fault; he's so good looking."

"Rebecca, this is our place of business. Will you stop it."

"I know where I am, Payton. Stop being so uptight. You're starting to sound like Abby."

"Whatever. Follow me."

I waved hello to Nancy at the front desk before making my way outside to talk with Rebecca privately.

"I'm not sure what you're doing here, but we agreed that I would talk to Dad, remember?"

"I know, but this morning I was thinking about it and decided maybe I could be of some help."

"Well, you can't right now. We already agreed that we wouldn't bombard him."

"I didn't want to bombard him ... I just thought..."

"How would you feel if the roles were reversed and both of your kids were approaching you about a conversation that one overheard?"

"True."

"Either way, Dad seems to be confident because he gave

Cole the go ahead for the renovation project. When the time is right I was going to gently bring it up."

"Okay, I was just trying to help."

"Don't worry. I'll keep an eye on it."

"On another note, tell me more about Cole."

"Don't you have somewhere to be? Like at a place called work?"

"I have a few minutes to spare. What's with you? Whatever happened to you being the fun middle sister that didn't behave like an old prude?"

"I don't know what that's supposed to mean, Becca. Nothing happened to me except life, I suppose. I grew up. I matured. We're not in college anymore. Yet, you're still acting like a wild bronco that needs to be tamed."

"I know we're not in college, but that doesn't mean we can't have fun. You and Abby found your guys. Even if it didn't work out, you had your shot at marriage. I was the one left behind while everyone else was off building their dream life."

"Please. Some dream life. My so-called dream life left me right where I started. Back in Pelican Beach."

"You're missing my point, Sis. I'm sorry your situation didn't work out for you. I really am. But at least you had an opportunity to go and make something of your life."

"You have the same opportunity, Becca. So far, from where I sit, you are making something of your life. Hello, Miss Lawyer, extraordinaire."

"That's just it. Since I wasn't able to find "the one," the least I could do was build a successful career. But my real heart's desire is to settle down and have a family."

"Have you ever considered your approach?"

"No, what's wrong with my approach?"

"It screams that you're desperate to meet someone. Wouldn't you rather let your relationships develop naturally?"

"I guess, but I don't see anything wrong with putting yourself out there."

"Well, I don't see anything wrong with getting to know someone without an agenda."

Rebecca seemed a little dismissive of the idea.

"Perspective is everything. I don't see it through the same lenses. I'm just making it known that I'm available for conversation. If it doesn't work out, then it doesn't work out."

"Okay, Miss Perspective. You have fun with that. I need to get back to work. Mom wants me to head over to the flower shop to take a look at some arrangements for the Inn."

"Alright. I guess I should be heading back as well. Keep me posted about Dad."

"Will do."

WILLIAM

I confess sometimes I have a habit of burying my head in the sand when it comes to work. Often times, I forget to come up for air. Helen hates it when I get overly consumed. If only she could see that I'm just trying to set up the best possible future for the family.

Everybody was out in the living room having a good time. I was in my usual location, the home office. Since today was a family day, I figured I would hurry along. If not, Helen would come looking for me.

"Will, we agreed this was going to be a relaxing weekend with the family. What are you doing?" She came looking for me just as expected.

"I won't be long. Just looking through some paperwork that I need to send over to the accountant. I also wanted to add on one or two more items for Cole to address in the renovations."

"Is Cole available to start soon?"

"Yep."

"Wonderful. The sooner he starts, the better. If he gets the lobby area finished in early July, then we'll have a beautiful new entrance for our busiest season of the year."

"That's the idea."

"Maybe we can have him start upgrading the rooms in the fall. You know, one section of the Inn at a time to go easy on the cost."

"Mmm-hmm."

"Will, speaking of the cost, how are the funds looking?"

"The numbers look fine to me. I have to meet with our accountant. He has his britches in a bunch about something. It's probably an oversight on his part. I plan on paying him a visit to set him straight."

"That doesn't sound good."

"Don't worry about a thing. I've done the finances for the Inn for as long as I can remember, and we've never had a problem."

"We certainly haven't. It still never hurts to have a second pair of eyes. We're so busy with day to day operations we could use the extra help."

"We have extra help. Why do you think I added new staff members this year?"

"I meant with the back end items that help keep things afloat."

"That's covered too, Helen." I knew my wife well enough to know that she was worrying. I got up and walked over to Helen and brushed her bangs to the side, before taking her into my arms.

"I don't want you to worry about this, Helen. We've worked so hard our entire lives. It's time to be able to relax and enjoy some of the fruit of our labor before we're not here to enjoy it anymore."

"I know, but..."

"I'm going to tell you like I told Payton. No buts!"

"Can I be frank with you, William?" She pulled back.

"Sure, you can. Nothing has ever stopped you before."

"I love our life at the Inn. I mean, yes, there's plenty of room for improvement to be made. We both could stand to slow down and smell the roses. But lately, you seem so stressed and frazzled. When I see you like that, I think it's no problem for me to step it up and help out more. We're in this together. We started this business together. We've had success, and hopefully, one day, we'll retire and live out our other dreams together."

"I like the way that sounds. In the meantime, I still want you to make me a promise not to worry so much. I'm fine, and the business is fine. I just want to see you and the girls happy."

"Me too. Speaking of being happy. What do you think about introducing Cole to Payton?"

Oh, here we go with my wife's other passion. I turned and started walking back toward my desk.

"Helen, I think that's a bad idea."

"Why? He's such a respectable gentleman, he has his own business, he's very talented, and he has a sweet little girl. I honestly don't see the problem."

"Cole is not the problem."

"Well, neither is Payton."

"I didn't say she was. You interfering in their business is the problem."

"I beg your pardon." She couldn't really do anything but smile because she knew I was right.

"You heard me. Payton is coming fresh out of a divorce and is in no position to be concerned with a new relationship. Cole is a father who has a little girl to look after. I'm sure his priority is making sure no one will come along and disrupt their happy home."

"There's more than one way to flip this coin, William Matthews, but I'll leave it alone for now."

"Yeah, right."

I've known her long enough to know better. I smirked and shook my head at her before returning to work.

"I'll be out in just a little bit to get the grill going."

Helen grunted as she returned to be with the kids.

PAYTON

*a*fter the festivities subsided at Mom and Dad's, the family sat around and shared old memories. Mom brought out a few photo albums for everyone to pass around.

Abby and Wyatt grabbed a glass of wine and laughed over pictures of when she was in Middle School. Rebecca and I admired photos of our parents leaning out of a car with a sign that read "just married."

"Those were the good old days, weren't they, Will?"

Dad sat in his recliner, looking a bit distracted. He was agreeing with mom but didn't seem too invested in the conversation.

"That's right, Honey."

After a few rounds of playing board games, most of us were ready to call it a night. However, dad lingered.

"How's it going, baby girl?" We were all "baby girl" in his eyes, no matter how old we are.

"It's going well, Dad. This was fun tonight. We should do it more often."

"We should. I honestly don't know where the time is going.

It seemed like we always had plans to have more family gatherings and trips, but we got busy and let time slip away from us."

"You're talking like we've run out of time. We can still plan gatherings and trips."

"Yes, but your dad is getting older. It's not quite the same."

I tried to search his eyes for the hidden meaning behind what he was saying.

"You want to join me for a walk?"

"Sure. After you."

It was a beautiful evening. The moonlight paved a bright pathway for an evening stroll along the beach. It seemed like dad had something weighing heavily on his heart.

"Payton, I've been wanting to talk with you about your role at the Inn. Ever since you told us you were returning to Pelican Beach, I thought it might be nice to get you involved in the family business again. Of course, those were my thoughts. I wanted to check with you about your plans."

"It's funny, I was just talking about this with Mom when we were at work on Friday. I promised that I would help out at the Inn. I figured it was the least I could do. You and Mom are being so gracious to let me come live with you for a while. In my spare time, I'd also like to work on building up my photography business. I was thinking that Pelican Beach is the perfect place to build a list of clients. We have the most gorgeous locations to take photos. Wedding photos, engagement photos, family photos, you name it."

"I see."

"You sound disappointed."

"It's not that, Honey." Dad looked down toward the sand as we continued to walk. I suspected there was something that was bothering him.

"What's wrong, Dad?"

"I need you to keep what I'm about to tell you between you and me until I'm ready to say something to the others."

"Of course."

"My mind doesn't seem to be as sharp as it once used to be."

"What are you talking about? Your mind is sharp as a tack."

"Hear me out, Payton. I get distracted and disoriented a lot. Your mother was the first one to bring it to my attention. To be honest, I used to get downright mad at her for doing it. But now I'm catching myself, and it's starting to worry me a little. I haven't said anything to your mother and I won't because I don't want her to worry. I don't even know that there's anything to worry about. But this is all the more reason that I need your help. At least for a little while until I get to the bottom of what's going on."

"Of course. Dad, you know I would do anything for you. Have you been to the doctor?"

"I have an appointment scheduled in two weeks. I couldn't get anything earlier. This doctor is one of the best."

"Okay, well, I'm happy to go with you for moral support."

"We'll see. I may tell your mother by then. I'm not sure yet. Either way, it would mean so much to have another family member around to help with day to day operations. With all three of us, there should be plenty of flexibility for you to still work on your photography."

"Sure, Dad. Just make me a promise."

"I'll try."

"Say something to Mom sooner rather than later, okay?"

"I will."

"And one more thing. While we're on the subject of the Inn. I accidentally picked up your telephone line and overheard part of a heated conversation with your accountant. I promise it wasn't my intention to pick up your line, but..."

"What did you hear?"

"Probably the worst part. He made it sound like you're in financial trouble and could be at risk for losing the Inn."

Dad faced the water and stared off into the darkness of the night. I knew I had struck a chord. I could feel the sand in between my toes as I waited nervously for him to respond. Perhaps the timing of my divorce and coming back home was all for a reason. Either way, I could only help as much as he was willing to let me.

WILLIAM

*M*y accountant Paul was rather new. Not to accounting, I made sure I researched his track record. But undoubtedly new to the way I do things. I went to his office and sat down with my briefcase filled with spreadsheets. At a moment's notice, I was ready to appeal any notion that the Inn was having financial trouble.

"Mr. Matthews, come on in. Let's have a seat at the table and talk. Can I offer you something to drink?"

"No, I'm fine, thank you. I don't have a lot of time this afternoon. I was hoping to get right down to the heart of things if that's okay with you."

"Sure, let's see what you have. I'll pull my numbers up here so we can go over everything together."

As he pointed his remote control toward a large screen, I was taking into consideration that sometimes I had a lot of trouble with my memory. It was frustrating to be quite honest, but I had gotten pretty good about going back and double-checking my work.

"After we spoke the other day, I went through the numbers

again, as I do every month. There were a couple of things I must've overlooked. But for the most part, we have a very healthy budget that includes more than enough wiggle room for renovations. Here, take a look for yourself."

Paul proceeded to look through the data, flipping the screen, month by month. He put on his glasses and combed through my numbers, continuously comparing it to what he had on the big screen. Not quite sure why he needed all the fancy technology to get the job done.

Truth be told, I was a little antsy, but I felt confident that his feedback wouldn't be anything less than stellar. Paul took his glasses off and sat back in his chair.

"At first glance, everything looks great. However, there's a major discrepancy between what you're presenting to me, and what I have in my records."

"What's the discrepancy?"

"Do you see here?"

Paul pointed on his screen toward a withdrawal for fifty thousand dollars.

"Then again here, another withdrawal in the amount of twenty-five thousand."

He continued to scroll through the information.

"How about over here."

He pointed to a few transfers. Some small amounts and other transfers that were much larger.

Paul turned to me and said, "How do you justify all of the transfers and withdrawals? Some of these transactions are being deposited into your account, but not hardly enough to make up for the deficit."

I tried to gather my thoughts. But before I could come up with anything, Paul continued.

"I know we haven't been working together too long. So I thought, surely you had some other accounts or files that you saved and wanted me to review with you today. If all we have to go by is the spreadsheet you brought in today, we're still in the red. Big time."

"Look. Occasionally I have to transfer funds in and out of some personal accounts, but I keep track of everything and have receipts to back it up."

"Sir, I'm sure you know it's bad practice to mix the business transactions with your personal. God forbid we were ever facing an audit. That would be a nightmare waiting to happen."

"I know, I know. Sometimes I get a little forgetful these days. But I swear I have all the receipts for each bank transaction. I brought them here with me today. Hold on."

The pressure was on. I started fumbling around in my bag, still convinced that the accountant was wrong, and this was a simple fix. I could feel the sweat penetrating my shirt underneath my arms.

"Here's what I can do for you, Mr. Matthews. I don't want you to have to sit here and scramble to get your receipts together under pressure. Leave the ones you have with me here today. You probably should look around for anything else you can dig up from the past year and send it my way as well."

I continued to frantically dig into the side pocket of my briefcase.

"Mr. Matthews?"

"Yes, yes. I heard you. You want me to go back and look for more receipts."

"More receipts and any other documents that can help me to better figure out what's really going on with your numbers here."

"Very well. I'll get everything over to you asap."

"Sounds good. In the meantime, I'd be cautious and hold off on any large expenses."

"Wait a minute. We signed a contract to start the renovations at the Inn. It begins this week, and I don't have any plans to abort the project just because of a little hiccup."

"A little hiccup? Sir, I don't know any other way to put this. According to what you're showing me, you're going to struggle to pay all of your bills soon if we don't solve this problem immediately. I hate to have to put it like this, but unless you have an endless supply of personal funds hidden somewhere, you need to put the renovations on hold."

It felt like the wind was sucked right out of my lungs. I sat back in the chair and let the glare from the sun rest on my face. The renovations were my big plan to attract more people to the Inn. We always had a steady flow of visitors, but if we were going to keep up with some of the neighboring Inns, we had to be able to offer the best. My original plans to do the renovations last year were set aside when Helen asked me to spruce up the Cottage. It was an anniversary gift, and I didn't want to disappoint. All the years of hard work, sweat, and tears. It was the least I could do to make her happy.

Back at the Inn, I called a meeting with Helen and Payton. It was time for me to lay everything on the table, plus I knew Helen would be curious to know.

"The accountant is right, Dad. You have to put the renovations on hold. There's no way to turn this thing around while taking on a new expense. You guys have a great relationship with Cole. I think we should reach out to him tonight and explain the circumstances. Perhaps we can agree to delay the project until we're able to rebound and get the budget back on track."

My wife and my daughter sat staring at me with a look of concern on their faces. This is exactly what I didn't want for them.

"Will, I just wish you would've said something to me. We've always supported each other. I could've helped you, Honey."

"I know you would've helped, Helen. I just wanted to take care of you the way I always have. It bothers me to see you working so hard and never taking time to enjoy our success."

"Well, I promise as soon as we get ourselves out of this mess, I'll take more time to enjoy. But in the meantime, we have to figure this thing out fast."

Payton stood up and paced around the room with her arms folded.

"What's on your mind, Payton?" Helen asked.

"I think I have an idea. Of course, I'll need to hear the final numbers from...what's the accountant's name again?"

"Paul."

"Yes, Paul. I'll need to hear the final numbers from him. Depending on what he says, I have some funds set aside from the sale of the house and our other assets. Jack didn't put up a fight. He let me have everything. I don't see why I can't use that money to help out my parents in a time of need."

I could feel myself getting hot. "Absolutely not! That's your money. You can use it to start your photography business or put down on another house. I won't hear of it."

"Dad. Hear me out. The Inn has proven itself over the years. You will make more than enough money to pay me back. This is just a temporary loan to get the bills all caught up to speed."

Helen spoke softly as she pleaded with me. "And it would relieve some stress so we can focus on taking better care of you, Dear. Please, William? Payton is right. We can pay her back."

I broke down in tears and finally lost control. I know my sobs echoed through the office. It was a tough pill to swallow, but in the end, it was our best option. How could I have screwed up like this?

Payton bent down beside my chair and handed me a handkerchief. "Do you want me to head over to Cole's shop before it gets too late?"

"Yes. Thank you, Payton. Please tell him I'll be in touch as soon as I can."

"No problem, Daddy."

She made her way to the door so Helen and I could have time alone.

"I'm going to head back to the house after I stop by Cole's. Call me if you need anything."

Helen thanked Payton again before she closed the door behind her. She then turned back to me.

"Will. I feel like there's more to this story. Is there anything else you want to share with me?"

"You already know what's going on, Helen. There's nothing to tell. You've watched me get frustrated and lose my train of thought on many occasions. My mind isn't working the way it used to. I was just being stubborn and never willing to admit it. I recently made an appointment to get it checked out. That's all. We'll have to wait and see what the doctor says."

I sat back in my chair, feeling defeated. Helen came over and placed my head against her chest. Lord knows I needed it. All I could do is cry and ask myself where I would be without this woman.

PAYTON

*L*ater that afternoon, I set out to see Cole. The drive to his office was a quiet one, as I tried to figure out what to say. I pulled down Main Street. This area of town is where most of the popular businesses were located along with the courthouse.

"What in the world?" My eyes couldn't believe who was parked out in front of Cole's shop.

"You have got to be kidding me!"

My sister's red convertible wasn't hard to miss, but I slowed down to read the rear tags just to be sure.

"That little..."

"Payton Matthews, keep your cool. The courthouse is right down the street. She's probably at work and just had to park further away today. Right? Right!"

I slammed the car door behind me, straightened out my pencil leg skirt, and checked my hair in the reflection of the car window. As I walked into the shop, I was greeted by the sound of a bell to announce my arrival.

The receptionist greeted me as I entered. "Welcome to

Pelican Renovations. May I help you?" Feeling relieved that Rebecca was nowhere in sight, I relaxed and tried to refocus on my reason for coming.

"Yes, my name is Payton Matthews. I'm here to see Cole Miller if he's available."

"Is he expecting you?"

Just then, Rebecca stepped out of the restroom with her bag resting on her forearm.

I was too busy staring at Rebecca to respond to the receptionist.

"Rebecca, fancy meeting you here."

The look of surprise on her face was priceless. She looked just like somebody who had been caught red-handed stealing from the candy jar.

"Hey, Sis. I didn't expect to see you here either."

I folded my arms and leaned against the counter.

"Well, that's funny because I could've sworn I told you about the renovation project for the Inn."

"Yes, about that. I was on my way back to my office when I saw Cole's name in the front window. I thought it was ironic that I hadn't noticed the place before, so I decided to stop in and say hello."

"Really?"

"As it turns out, he's not here anyway. So I was just using the powder room and now..."

She looked down at her watch.

"Ooh, it's getting late. I need to head back to the office."

"Oh, I bet."

Rebecca thanked the receptionist for allowing her to use the restroom and made her way out the front door. Just before she let the door close, she glanced up at me one last time. If looks could kill Rebecca would be toast.

I redirected my attention toward the receptionist, still feeling hot over the exchange.

"I apologize. I guess it's such a small town you're bound to run into somebody you're related to."

The receptionist gave me a blank stare, so I decided to continue on.

"I think you were asking me about an appointment."

"Yes, do you have one?"

"I don't. However, I have to touch base with Mr. Miller regarding the Matthews project. He's supposed to get started later this week, and there's been a slight change in plans."

"I'll have to take down your information and have him give you a call. He's not expected to return for another hour or so."

"Sure. Please let him know that it's urgent."

The bells rang as the door to the shop opened again. Cole walked in and greeted me with a big smile.

"Payton Matthews. I didn't expect to see you here today. How can I help you?"

If I was being honest, there was something about his smile that almost made me forget why I came. "Mr. Miller. Just the man I was looking for."

"Please call me Cole. Is everything alright?"

"Not quite. If you have a minute, I'd like to chat with you about the project."

"Absolutely. Why don't you step into my office so we can talk?"

"Thank you."

Cole stopped by his receptionist's desk and picked up his messages. "Martha, if you wouldn't mind holding my calls until I'm done meeting with Miss Matthews, that would be great."

"You got it."

I noticed Martha looking up at me over the top of her bifocals. Her head slowly turned to watch me as I walked by. I'm almost certain that whole scene with my sister peeked her curiosity.

Once inside his office, I admired the awards and accolades hanging on the wall.

"Wow, I know Mom and Dad rave about your work, but I didn't realize how accomplished you are. My goodness."

"Why, thank you. I'd like to think even without all the recognition that my craftsmanship speaks for itself."

"It does. My parents' house looks absolutely beautiful."

"Please, make yourself comfortable."

I took a seat across from his desk and started to feel awful about what I was about to say.

"So, what brings you to my office today?"

"Well, there's no good way to say this, so I'll just come right out with it. Unfortunately, there has been a major hiccup with the financing for this project. My father..."

I hesitated for a moment.

"You can talk to me, Payton. I've known your father for years. He's a well-respected businessman in the community."

"That's what makes this even more challenging. We don't want to lose your respect. However, my father recently had a meeting with his accountant. He advised him not to continue with the project at this time. Apparently, there are a few concerns with the accounts that need to be squared away to ensure that business can continue to run smoothly."

"Wow, I wasn't aware."

"None of us were aware. Not even Dad. I hope you know that he would've never booked the renovation with you if he truly believed there was a problem."

Cole scratched his head.

"Is there something I can do?"

"I wish. Between the two of us, I suspect whatever is going on has been going on for a little while now. I'm confident we'll get the finances in order. However, Dad's been complaining about feeling forgetful and just seems more flustered than usual. Getting him in to see the doctor is more of a concern to me than anything else. He's always handled the finances and kept the business running without a hitch."

"I can imagine. We have some of the finest doctors in the area. I'm sure they can see him and get to the bottom of what's going on."

"He's scheduled to go in soon."

"Good. Please keep me posted if you don't mind. I've always thought of your folks as more than just clients. Let me know how things turn out."

"Absolutely."

"In the meantime, I guess you need me to release you from the contract?"

My eyes scanned downward toward my lap. "Yes, if you wouldn't mind. I feel awful having to ask."

"Payton." As he stared at me with his light blue eyes, I could tell that he was sincere.

"Please do not worry about this. I'll be here when you're ready."

"Thank you, Cole. I promise we will give you a call as soon as things are back to normal."

Cole extended his hand across the desk. "You have a deal."

He stopped in the middle of a hardy handshake and said, "Wait. A deal is never really official unless it includes having an ice cream cone after."

While still holding hands, I broke out into laughter. "I wasn't expecting that one. An ice cream cone makes it official?"

"What? You didn't know?"

"I didn't have the slightest clue, but the offer sounds hard to refuse. You got yourself a deal."

I'm not going to lie, I wondered for just a moment if Cole

was interested in me. But in the end, I think he was just being kind. I was certain of it.

On the way walking back to the front, I smiled at Martha again.

"Thanks again for your help today, Martha."

"No problem, Dear."

"Martha, I'm running around the corner with Miss Matthews. I'll be back shortly. If Emmie calls, please tell her to reach me on my cell phone."

Martha looked beyond the trim of her glasses at us. "Okay, Boss. I'll see you, laterrrrr."

Cole shook his head and snickered on the way out the door.

"Martha is more like a family member than an employee. Even though it's not part of her job description, she is protective over me when it comes to the ladies. Whenever eager, single women slither in, she has a way of keeping them in line. If she likes the person, she sings a different tune."

If that's the case, I don't think Rebecca scored very well. Then again, the way I spoke to her in front of Martha probably didn't help.

"Just past the dock, there's this little creamery that has a lot of delicious options."

"Sounds good. It's been a while since I've taken a leisurely stroll down Main Street, so this is a nice treat."

"We couldn't ask for a more beautiful day, that's for sure."

"Hey, Cole. Listen, before we go any further I have a confession to make."

"Uh, oh."

"It's not bad. At least I don't think it is. I normally make it a habit to keep things strictly professional. You know the whole mixing business with pleasure thing. It doesn't usually go over so well."

"I'm sorry. Did my invitation to ice cream make you uncomfortable?"

"No, no. Not at all. Going for ice cream was the least I could do after having to break a contract with you. I'm so grateful that you were understanding."

"Of course. I know your parents will come through with other jobs when they can. They're good people. Plus, I'd be lying if I didn't admit that my schedule is pretty slammed. I didn't want to tell your dad no, but I could use a little wiggle room over the next couple of weeks."

"Oh, well, now I feel much better."

"I told you not to feel bad. But getting back to your confession. What's on your mind?"

"Yes, my confession." We paused where the boats were docked and locked eyes for a moment.

"My sister would probably kill me for saying this, so pinky-swear that you won't tell her?"

Cole locked pinkies with me, demonstrating his loyalty.

"Rebecca stopped by to say hello to you before you walked into the shop. I think she might be interested in you."

"You think?"

I knew I wasn't the only one watching her make a fool over herself!

"Is it obvious?"

"Pretty much."

"Well, take it easy on her. She's still trying to find her way. Normally I don't get involved in her business. However, this time I asked her to ease up a bit because my parents have a professional relationship with you. Needless to say, it didn't go over so well. I think I may have encouraged the opposite."

"Yikes."

"I know. Anyway, she works right here on Main Street. So

heaven forbid she sees us, as innocent as it may be, I'll never hear the end of it!"

"Gotcha. Wow, that's too bad. So I guess that asking you out to dinner would be completely out of order?"

I didn't quite know how to respond.

"I mean...for one it's breaking your rule regarding professionalism. Then there's the whole thing with your sister."

"Umm, yeah. It's just... you know. Messy."

"Right," Cole responded.

I wanted to kick myself. On the one hand, the last thing I needed to be thinking about was going on a date after the whirlwind of a divorce. But on the other hand, Cole seemed like a nice guy, and I was curious to know more about him. Then there was Rebecca.

"I'm sorry, Cole."

"Hey, no apologies needed. I completely understand. It was ridiculous of me to bring it up."

I regretted creating such an awkward moment.

"It wasn't ridiculous at all. Truth be told, you wouldn't want to be bothered with a girl like me. I come with way too much baggage."

"Don't we all?"

"I don't know. I never imagined that I'd wait until my forties to have everything in my world flipped upside down. I thought I'd have it all together by now. Or at least I thought I'd be better off."

"That's just it, Payton. We never dream about having baggage. It's not like you wrote in your diary as a young girl "When I grow up, I want to have lots and lots of baggage.""

I had to laugh at that one. He had a good point.

"Lord, no. I certainly did not!"

"I know you didn't. Neither did I. It's an unfortunate part of life, but it doesn't have to define us. It certainly shouldn't stop us from living our lives. It took me many years to learn that lesson after my wife passed away."

"I'm sorry. I can imagine it's not easy recovering from something like that."

"She would've never wanted me walking around carrying so much emotional baggage. Drowning myself in my sorrows for as long as I did was not a part of the plan. I'm not saying you shouldn't have a period to grieve. But make sure it's only for a season. Then give yourself permission to move on."

I took Cole's words to heart. As a little girl, I may have dreamt of happily ever after, but things didn't turn out that way in my marriage with Jack. That didn't mean that all hope was lost. It felt uplifting to know that I didn't have to carry around the baggage from a broken marriage forever.

HELEN

*B*reakfast on Saturday mornings had become a thing between my girls and me. This morning, in particular, Rebecca was busy and wasn't able to join us.

"Morning, Mom." Abby greeted me with a kiss.

"Morning, Love. Where are my grand babies?"

"I let them hang out with their dad this morning. Wyatt rarely gets to have alone time with them. They'll be here to pick me up later."

"Hey, Ab." Payton was sipping OJ, waiting for Abby's arrival.

"Would you look at this pretty blue sky! I don't think there's a cloud in sight. We can't let this day go by without getting down to the beach."

I didn't waste any time digging into my scrambled eggs.

"I'd love to, but I don't think your father is feeling up to it this morning."

"How's Dad taking the news?" Abby asked.

"I don't think he knows how to react. None of us do. The

last thing we expected the doctor to say was that he's showing early signs of dementia."

"Yeah, but there's medication that can help, right?"

"Abby, you know your father. He's always been able to do everything on his own. Always had a sharp mind. Medication or not, it's going to take a while to adjust to something like this."

"You seem to be taking it rather well."

"I've had my moments. But your father has always been strong for me. Now it's my turn to do the same for him."

Payton placed her hand over my hands. She's always had a compassionate soul. "It's going to be okay, Mom. We'll still make sure Dad's involved as much as he wants to be. We'll do whatever it takes to support him."

"This is the busiest season of the year. Who's going to run the Inn?" Abby seemed concerned.

"Your father and I have been running the Inn together for years. What am I chopped liver?"

"No, of course not. But doing it all by yourself?"

"No, not by myself. As Payton mentioned, we're going to keep your father involved as much as possible, and she's going to help out as well."

Abby glanced over at Payton.

"And what's going to happen with your dream of starting the photography business?"

"I'll be putting all that on hold temporarily. This is not a forever plan, but right now, Mom and Dad need help. You have the kids to look after, and Rebecca has her career."

"Even if she didn't have her career, Rebecca would still find a way to do her own thing."

That was my cue to jump in and interrupt Abby's rant.

"Leave your sister alone. She has a lot on her plate."

"Mmm, hmm. She has a lot on her plate, alright. Somehow

she always finds a way to make time for what she thinks is important. You may not want to admit it, Mom, but it's true."

Sometimes I wished my girls wouldn't go at it with each other so much.

"Abby has a point there, Mom. Did I tell you about my little run-in with her at Cole's shop?"

"No."

Payton had our full attention.

"Oh yeah. It was a classic Rebecca moment. This was around the time that I had to talk to him about canceling the renovation project. I stopped by to meet with him and who comes walking out of the restroom, but Becca."

"What was she doing there?"

"She said she noticed his name in the window and decided to stop in to say hello. Her little plan backfired on her when she found out he wasn't there."

"Wait. This doesn't even make sense. How does Rebecca know Cole?"

"She met him briefly when she stopped by the Inn. Brief as in he walks up to say goodbye, she asks, "who's this handsome man?" Then her eyes follow him out the door. And apparently now she's head over heels. I probably started something by giving her a pep talk about keeping things professional. Next thing I know, I'm running into her at his shop."

I couldn't help but shake my head in confusion. It just didn't make sense. "I've always wondered why Rebecca hasn't settled down with a nice man. She has so much to offer. She's young, and she has a law degree, I just don't understand. The right guy is out there for her. Although I don't know that Cole is the one, he's much more your speed, Payton."

"Mom, Cole is a business associate, and I'm not looking for another relationship right now."

"Who said anything about business or relationships?

There's nothing wrong with getting to know him is all I was trying to suggest."

Abby appeared to be getting a kick out of my comment from the smirk on her face.

"Well, speaking of getting to know him, he actually tried to ask me to dinner, but I declined."

"Why would you do a thing like that?"

"Umm, hello? It wasn't long ago that I was slamming the door in Jack's face. You witnessed it. Don't you think I have enough drama going on in my life right now?"

Abby held up one finger to object. "If I may say something here. Technically you have nothing going on right now except for working at the Inn. Other than that, your schedule is pretty open."

"Very funny, Abby."

"It's true. I'm not trying to be funny. So tell us all the details. When did he ask you out, and what did he say?"

"It's not a big deal. I guess he could tell I was feeling bad about having to break the contract. He told me not to and said that he understood. One thing led to another, we shook on it, and he invited me to take a walk down to the creamery. That's it. It was just a kind gesture."

"Kind gesture, alright!" I wasn't buying it. I'd lived long enough to know when a man was interested in a woman.

"If it was just a kind gesture, why did it lead to an invitation for dinner?"

"Good point," Payton said.

"I told your father he'd be a nice guy for you to meet."

"You said that to Dad?"

"Yep, I sure did. Mother always knows best."

Abby laughed. "Perhaps Mom should start a matchmaking service on the side."

"I'd be pretty darn good at it too."

"Guys, can we be serious here?"

"I am serious about Cole," I responded.

"Stop being such a prude. Learn to live a little. Have fun. You only have one life, Payton. Might as well live it to the fullest."

Abby bounced up. "So here's what we have to do. We have to find a way to get Cole over to the house. You know, to give him and Payton a second chance to talk."

"Here we go." Payton threw her hands up in the air.

"I don't know that your father's up for a party at the house right now, Abby."

"Okay, then. What about Luau night? You're having the annual Luau night at the Inn next weekend, right?"

"Now that you mention it, that's a great idea. All of the locals usually stop by for Luau night. I'll give him a call and ask him to bring Emmie and his mother. It will be so much fun."

"In case you two haven't noticed, I'm still sitting here. I love how you have this all figured out. But have you forgotten that Rebecca has a crush on Cole? And did I mention I'm not looking for a man?"

"I'll take care of your sister. Just be sure to show up with your leis on and get ready to have some fun."

"You two are unbelievable. Abby, you are no help at all, egging Mom on like that."

"I think she's right. It's time for you to start living again, Payton. Life's too short."

"He is kinda cute."

"See. That's my girl. There's nothing wrong with letting your hair down and living a little. If I knew right, it was probably just what the doctor ordered."

"Mom, let me preface this by saying I don't mean any harm, but I have to ask Payton this question." Abby shifted toward Payton.

"Are you sure you want to get so heavily involved with running the Inn? That's quite the undertaking and quite a derailment from your dreams."

"You're right. It's not my ultimate dream. I've always envisioned myself staying at an Inn on vacation, not running one. But if I don't step in and help, then what will Mom and Dad do?"

"You're right. They do need the help. All I'm saying is while you're helping, make sure you keep your eyes on your dreams too."

"I will."

"You know how easy it is to get sucked in. Don't forget. I used to work at the Inn before I had Maggie."

I tried to help Abby see the bright side of things. "But that was back before we hired more staff, Abby. Having the extra help does make a difference."

"True."

"Don't worry. We will all help to keep Payton's dreams at the forefront. This is just a temporary solution."

We really didn't mean to get Payton roped in to this degree, to begin with. It's incredible how quickly things spiraled out of control. I do want to see her succeed at reaching her dreams. I remember first-hand what it was like to accomplish ours.

"On another note, I have some fun news to share." Payton sat up with excitement.

"I found a sweet little house to rent on the other side of Pelican Beach."

"Aw Payton, that's wonderful, Darling!"

"Thanks. You guys should come check it out with me if you have time. The landlord is freshening up the paint and doing a few odds and ends. After it's finished, they said I could stop by to take a final look before signing the lease."

"Sure, I'll check with Wyatt and see which days he's working from home." Abby volunteered.

"Payton, we'll both go with you. I can't wait to see it."

"Aunt Payton, Aunt Payton!" Sweet little voices came running from inside.

"Speaking of the kids. Look who's here."

"Ooh, come here and give Aunt Payton a hug."

"Aunt Payton isn't the only one sitting at the table. You better come over here and give your Gram a kiss."

Wyatt joined the ladies to catch up on everything with the family.

PAYTON

On the eve of the Luau, the guests made their way to the veranda to enjoy the festivities. The locals and guests at the Inn visited throughout the day to participate in pass the coconut, volleyball on the beach, eating, and live entertainment.

"Everything looks fantastic. Compliments to the chef for bringing the taste of Hawaii to the Inn," Claire said.

"Thank you, Claire. It's so good to see you. How's the store coming along?"

Claire was the owner of "Claire's Fashion" on the Northern end of Pelican Beach.

"I can't complain. Of course, this is our busy time of the year, so I'm sure none of the owners are complaining right about now."

"You have a good point. It seems like we have even more guests than usual this year."

"How are Helen and William doing?"

"They're good. I'm sure they're somewhere around here

mingling with everyone. You should go and say hello. They'd love to see you."

"I will, but first I'm going grab a cocktail."

"Please do. Enjoy something tropical for the two of us!"

"I most certainly will. Glad to have you back, Payton! We've missed you."

"Thank you, Claire."

I made my way over to greet Abby and Wyatt as they arrived with the kids.

"Leis for the lovely ladies and gentlemen."

"Thank you, Sis. Kids, what do you say to your Aunt Payton?"

"Thank youuuu."

"You're welcome. Why don't you go find Gram and Poppa to let them know you're here."

"Okay."

The kids ran off to find their grandparents while Wyatt and Abby stayed back to chat with me.

"Look at you with your Hawaiian flower in your hair and your beautiful sundress."

"Do you like it? I tried to get into the Aloha spirit."

Wyatt spoke on their behalf. "Well, you did a beautiful job not only on your outfit but with everything. This is always a fun event, but the extra touches you added this year are amazing."

"Aww, thanks, Wyatt. Back when things were good, Jack and I used to spend a lot of time in Maui. I think a little bit of the Hawaiian tradition rubbed off on me."

"It sure did. I love the torches. It's so romantic. Wyatt, we should've found a sitter. I'm in the mood for a date night."

"You're right, Honey. We are long overdue for a date night!"

"I'll come babysit so you two can get out and have fun."

Abby spotted Cole coming with Emmie and his mother.

"We'll take you up on that offer. In the meantime, don't look now, but Cole is coming, and it looks like he has company," Abby whispered.

"How do I look?"

"Stunning. I'm just not sure if you're wearing your flower on the right side. Isn't it supposed to be on the right side if you're single?"

"Abby, do you really think anybody's paying attention to the position of my flower? We're in Pelican Beach for goodness sake. And why are we whispering?"

"I have no idea. We're going to hurry so you two can talk. See ya."

No matter what he wore, Cole looked like a natural model for a fitness magazine. He approached me with a young girl beside him who had the sweetest baby blue eyes just like her dad. She had her hair in a ponytail and a Hawaiian style dress. Her fingernails were painted every color of the rainbow, and she had a flower in her hair, keeping in line with the theme.

"Are you Miss Payton?"

"Yes, I am. And you are?"

"I'm Emmie. My dad told me to give these to you to say thank you for having us."

"Aren't you precious? What a sweet gift."

I looked up toward Cole. "You didn't have to do this. Your invitation was free of charge."

"I know I didn't have to, but I wanted to."

"Well, thank you. Peonies are my absolute favorite." I then turned back to Emmie.

"You outdid yourself, young lady."

"There's someone else I'd like you to meet. This is my mother, Alice Miller."

"Mrs. Miller, it's so nice to meet you."

"Likewise. I've heard so many wonderful things about the Inn and about you. It's nice to finally meet you."

"You couldn't have chosen a better time to visit. Our Luau night is usually the talk of the town."

"From the looks of things, I can see why."

"Well, please make yourself at home, grab a plate of food, and enjoy."

"I certainly will." She turned to Cole and gave him the cue to stay and talk. "Son, if you're looking for Emmie and me, we'll be over by the dancers."

"Alright, Mom. Take it easy out there."

"Don't you worry about me. I knew how to shake a leg or two back in my day."

Cole looked wide eyed at me. "Oh, boy."

"Hey, leave your mother alone. She sounds like a lady who knows how to have a good time."

"She does, actually. She always adds so much fun and warmth to the house whenever she stays with us."

"Does she live in the area?"

"She lives about forty minutes north of Pelican Beach. She's considering moving since she spends so much time helping with Emmie. We haven't really worked out the details yet, but we'd both love it if she moved closer."

"I'm sure that would be nice."

"How about you? Have you thought about where you might settle?"

"I found a nice little rental on the other side of Pelican Beach. I'm going to visit again next week just to be certain. It's so pricey out here. I want to make the wisest choice and not be too far away from my parents."

"Will you continue to work here at the Inn?"

"That's the plan. For now, at least."

"Do I hear a little hesitation in your voice? You're already a hit among the people here. I can't imagine why this wouldn't be a good fit for you."

"It's not really a hesitation. I just have some other things my heart is set on pursuing while I help out at the Inn."

"Oh, do tell."

"It's a long story. I'm just like any other person with big dreams. Dreams that may never go any further than the pages of my journal."

"Hang on, not so fast. If it's a passion of yours, I don't see why it wouldn't leap off the pages of your journal and turn into something more."

Call it a nervous reaction, but I laughed it off as if it were no big deal. Deep down inside, I knew better.

"Do you have time to take a walk? I'd love to hear more about this big dream of yours."

"Oh, man. Now I feel like I'm being put on the spot."

"Not really. I just happen to know a thing or two about following dreams, so maybe I can be of some help to you. If you want."

"Alright. Let me go and put the flowers in water, and I'll be right back."

"I'll be right here waiting for you."

I made my way through the crowd to let my parents know I was going to be back in a little while. Then I brought the flowers to the kitchen to place the flowers in a vase.

"Miss Payton, your ideas for Luau night turned out to be quite a success."

"Aww, thank you, Shelby. Hey, I thought we agreed on you calling me Payton?"

"I'm sorry, you're right."

"I've never been formal with our employees a day in my life, and I'm not going to start now."

"I promise, from now on, Payton it is."

"Ok, that's much better. Make sure you grab yourself a plate of food, Shelby. I'll be back in just a little bit if anybody is looking for me."

"Sounds good."

After taking a deep breath, I made my way back to the party. I felt like a young girl discovering I liked a boy for the first time. Unfortunately, when I spotted Cole, the view in front of me was quite disturbing. Another woman stood rather close with her hand on his chest. Cole didn't exactly pull away. The woman was wearing a short skimpy dress and looked like something out of a trashy movie scene.

"You know we have some unfinished business, Cole. You and me. How about you stop by my place later tonight."

Cole looked up toward me, but it was already too late. Feeling uncomfortable, I turned around, and made my way out of the Inn. I could hear him calling me from behind.

"Payton. Payton. Wait. Please stop. I can explain."

"That's what they all say, Cole. Leave me alone."

"What do you mean?"

"Men. That's what they all say when they're doing something they should be ashamed of."

"But I wasn't doing anything that I'm ashamed of. Right before you came, she walked up to me."

"You didn't exactly look like you were turning her down. Wait a minute. I don't even know why I care. You don't owe me any explanations."

"Payton."

"Seriously. You don't owe me any explanations, Cole. It's not like we're..."

"What?"

"Nothing."

"Say it."

"Look. You seem like a really nice guy."

"Oh, here we go. The nice guy speech. Please spare me the nice guy speech. I know I don't owe you an explanation, but I want to give you one anyway, so just listen. I worked with her boss on a renovation project that I completed last year. She tried to come on strong back then, and I turned her down. I haven't seen the woman since then. I swear nothing is going on with us or any other woman for that matter. There's only one woman I'm interested in, Payton, and that's you."

His words disarmed a bit. I wanted to believe him but didn't know what to say.

"Come on, Payton. I'm a family man with a young child to raise. Does she look like the type of woman I would want around my daughter?"

"I would hope not for Emmie's sake."

"There's that smile. I was afraid you were about to kick me to the curb."

"I'm sorry about the way I reacted. This just proves what I was trying to tell you the other day. I have baggage from my past, and apparently, I'm still raw from it."

"And what did I tell you in response? We all have baggage. Don't we?"

"Yes."

Cole extended his hand to me.

"You can trust me. I promise I'm not going to make a fool of you or play with your heart."

"I'm still getting to know you, Cole."

"Fair enough. In the spirit of getting to know each other, let's take this walk down the beach." We took our shoes off and walked along the beach under the bright moonlit sky. The high tide sent crashing waves over our feet, but it felt good on such a hot summer evening.

"So tell me about this big dream of yours. What do you really want to do?"

I considered whether or not I should share but decided to take a leap of faith.

"I'm a photographer at heart. I haven't had a chance to use my equipment since I returned to Pelican Beach. Everything's all packed away in storage, and it's just as well because I've been pretty busy at the Inn. When I was married, I worked as a freelance photographer, and I thoroughly enjoyed every minute of it. It was my escape from everything that was falling apart in my life. Taking pictures in places with scenic views and watching people experience such joy from the photos filled my cup. It was my passion, my gift, and in a lot of ways, it provided comfort during a time when I felt so broken."

"That's amazing. Have you ever thought of starting your own photography business?"

"Have I? Only a thousand times. I can totally see myself setting up a shop and consulting with my clients over their photos. I've even sketched out plans about the different kinds of party and wedding packages I could offer."

"So, you just want to photograph weddings and parties?"

"Oh, no. Weddings, graduations, retirement parties, destination events. The sky is the limit. One time I visited this photography shop that was set up in an old house built in the 1920s. The place was completely renovated on the inside to look like an old parlor. It gave me that cozy feeling of visiting at someone's home while looking through photo albums and pictures. I'd love to create something special like that."

"Wow, it seems like you've put a lot of thought into this."

"I have. Photography is so much more to me than just taking a picture. It's capturing a moment in time that you can never get back. It's hearing my client's vision and bringing it to fruition. I get excited just thinking about it."

"You know the only way to satisfy that yearning on the inside is to put your dreams into action."

"I don't disagree with you. It's just ... right now, timing is everything."

I turned to the water and allowed the wind to blow through my hair.

"Enough about me. Are you living out your dreams?"

"For the most part, I'd say so. I've always wanted to be a father, so I consider it a blessing to have Emmie. I just never envisioned this version where my child would be without a mother. As for the business, I always knew I was good with my hands. Starting the renovation company was like a dream come true. Now that we've expanded, it's even better."

"I can tell it's your passion. Thinking back to the day you were taking measurements in the front lobby, you definitely looked like a man who was on a mission."

Cole laughed.

"No, seriously. You didn't even realize I was standing there waiting to get your attention."

"Yep. That's about right. Hey, I love what I do. What can I say?"

Cole looked deep into my eyes. I was tempted to lean in closer to him. Instead, I quietly cherished the moment wishing it would never end.

"You think we should head back to the Inn?" Cole asked.

"We probably should. I'm sure my parents could use an extra hand with the guests. This was a nice little break. I enjoyed it."

"Did you enjoy it enough to join me for dinner?"

"Cole Miller, you are one persistent man, aren't you?"

"Only if I think it's worth it."

I avoided making the same mistake twice. "I'd love to join you for dinner."

"Really? I thought surely you might shoot me down again."

"I can change my answer if you want me to." I teased.

"No, no, we're good. As a matter of fact, let's seal the deal before you change your mind. Do you have plans on Thursday evening?"

"No, I don't think so."

"Okay, well, there's this new place in town called The Cove. I heard they have great food and play music outdoors if you're interested in going."

"I'd love to go."

"It's a date then."

As we returned to the Inn, we ran into Rebecca in the front lobby.

"Payton, do you have a minute?"

I could tell from the tone of her voice this wasn't going to be good.

"Sure."

I followed Rebecca to the conference room in the back. As soon as the door shut behind me she began to let me have it.

"Would you mind explaining to me what I just saw outside?"

She caught me off guard by raising her voice at me.

"I don't know. What did you see?"

"You've got to be kidding me. You must think I was born yesterday, Payton. I saw you two walking together like a couple. I saw you giggling and looking at each other with that look. You know the look I'm talking about."

I could tell she was ticked off but the way she was coming at me was comical. It felt like she was fighting for her man. Except last time I checked she didn't have a man.

"Rebecca, are you going to let me talk to you? Or are you just going to keep yelling at me?"

"What could you possibly have to say. I already saw you with my own eyes. The nerve of you to think..."

Just then Mom swung open the door and gave the two of us a look.

"What on God's green earth is going on in here?"

I looked at Rebecca. I thought perhaps she'd like to explain since she was the one making all the loud fuss.

"Don't look at me like that," Rebecca said. "You're the one who has some explaining to do."

Mom closed the door and asked, "Explaining about what?"

"Well, Mom." I started walking around the room to keep from going off on Rebecca.

"Rebecca brought me back here to ever so loudly ask me what I was doing outside with Cole."

"Don't do that, Payton. Don't make it look like I'm the one to blame. You gave me this whole talk about being professional, and not putting myself out there. Now I see it was just because you wanted Cole for yourself."

"It's not like that at all, Rebecca."

Mom jumped in before we could go any further. "I've heard just about enough. The both of you sit down."

"But..." Rebecca tried to get a word in but Mom wasn't having it.

"Sit down."

The three of us took a seat at the conference table.

"Rebecca, your sister didn't do anything wrong."

"How are you taking sides with her?" Rebecca said.

"Hold it. Let me finish. A few weeks back Payton actually refused Cole's invitation to dinner because of you and her commitment to being a professional. I encouraged her to do otherwise because I think they would make a good match."

Rebecca's eyes bulged in disbelief and I felt like hiding under the table.

"So this was a team effort?"

"No, of course not. Would you listen to yourself? A team

effort to do what, Rebecca? Steal your boyfriend? No! For goodness sake. You don't even know Cole Miller. And if you did, you'd probably lose interest."

"What makes you say that?"

"Because I've actually spent time with the guy. When he did the renovations at the cottage I got to know him pretty well. Did you know one of his favorite hobbies is to go fishing?"

"No."

"Of course you don't. And you hate anything that has to do with fish. Here's a good one. Did you know he has a daughter named Emmie?"

"No."

"Hmm. How many times have you told me that the idea of having kids is not for you for many years to come. Maybe years after you're married you said. Did you know..."

"Okay, Mom. I get it."

"Do you? Because I could go on."

I wanted to hear more but I didn't dare say anything. Besides, Mom was on a roll and Rebecca was starting to have that look of regret in her eyes.

"You don't have to go on. I believe you. I still think Payton could've said something to me."

I placed my hand on hers. "You're right. I let time slip away without saying anything and I'm sorry for that. However, everything Mom told you is true."

Mom wasn't finished yet. "This is your sister, Rebecca. Not some random stranger. Next time give her the benefit of the doubt before going after her like that."

"Yes, Ma'am."

"Of course I'm expecting there won't be a next time. I'll consider all that yelling in our place of business to be a temporary moment of insanity. Hopefully now you've come back to your senses?"

Rebecca and I looked at each other and laughed. Mom was pretty funny with her analogies. However, we both knew she meant business.

"Well, good. That's behind us and now we can finish taking care of our guests."

Rebecca turned to me. "Okay, so I was being a little jealous."

"Oh my, was that an apology?" I teased.

"I'm sorry... Annnnd... you guys actually do look cute together, Pay."

"Thanks, Sis."

I still kind of wanted to knock her into next week but I'll keep those thoughts to myself. Sisterhood. What can I say? Even as adults we still quarrel sometimes but we still love each other just the same.

PAYTON

"$\mathcal{I}$t's rare that Mom and Dad would be home at noon on a weekday. I wonder what's going on?" Abby paced around the living room as we waited for Rebecca to arrive.

"I'm not sure what's going on, but they've been off their normal routine for the last couple of days."

"You guys live and work together. I'm surprised you don't know what's going on."

"Abby, at times, it gets so busy at the Inn we barely have time to speak."

"True. Hey, you never called me about seeing the rental this week. Whatever happened with that?"

"I completely forgot to tell you that the landlord called and said he ran into a few issues with the repairs. He's not going to be able to rent the place out for another month."

"Oh, that's too bad."

"Initially, that's what I was thinking. But maybe I dodged a bullet if the place needs that many repairs."

Mom and Dad joined us in the living room, followed by Rebecca, who just arrived from work.

"This must be pretty important if we're having a family meeting." Rebecca was just as curious and clueless as the rest of us.

Dad began to explain while Mom sat by his side.

"I should start by saying we wanted you all here today because we're about to make a big decision that will impact the future of the Inn."

We looked at each other with expressions of deep concern.

"Your mother and I have thought long and hard about this, and we wanted you to hear everything from us first. Helen, would you like to tell them?"

"We've decided to put the Inn up for sale. We have a meeting with the realtor this afternoon to go over the details."

"What?" I was shocked.

Abby and Rebecca sat on the couch with blank stares. After us, the Inn had always been near and dear to their hearts.

"Trust me when I tell you this decision wasn't an easy one to make. We always thought we'd be able to keep the Inn and pass it down to the next generation of kids or grandkids."

I had to ask about the obvious. "Is it Dad's health?"

"Yes and no, Honey. That has a lot to do with it, but it's not the entire reason. Initially, I thought we would still carry on, and your father could work as much or as little as he wanted to. Depending on how he felt, of course. I assumed that would be enough to keep things afloat. But now that we've had time to really think things over, it's just not a realistic plan."

"What you're mother is trying to say is we're getting older, and we want to get out there and enjoy our lives before we get to the place where we can't anymore. As for my health, some days are great. Just as if nothing were wrong. Other days are more frustrating and challenging. As it continues to progress,

73

we want to be able to give our full attention to taking care of those needs without the stress of the business on our shoulders. Trust me. This wasn't an easy decision, but we think it's best. Hopefully, it makes sense to you."

"It makes sense, it's just so sad. Ever since I was a little girl, this is all you've ever done," Rebecca responded.

"I know, Sweetheart. I like to think of it as bittersweet. While it's the completion of one era, the idea of having the freedom to do other things is something to look forward to as well."

Then Dad addressed me. "This also would be an opportunity for us to pay back any of the remaining funds we owe you and for you to start focusing on your dreams."

"Dad, your health is what's most important to me. The rest will fall in line in due time."

"Thank you, Sweetheart."

"There's only one thing left to do at a time like this." All eyes shifted to Rebecca as she stood to raise her hand. "Let's celebrate. Who wants a glass of wine?"

"Really, Rebecca. Is that all you can come up with?" Abby rolled her eyes.

Mom encouraged Abby to look at the bright side. "What's wrong with making a toast to new beginnings?"

"She has a point, Abby. We don't have to sit around here in mourning like somebody just died. If Mom and Dad are happy with the decision, we should be happy too. You heard your father. It's a new era," I agreed.

"That's the spirit, everyone." Rebecca riled everyone up to celebrate but not before putting Abby in her place.

"I have to tell you, Abby, you might be the oldest sister, but you have a lot of growing up to do. You never miss an opportunity to belittle whatever I say. But today's not about you or me. It's about Mom and Dad. Grow up."

Abby opened her mouth as if she were going tear her to pieces but thought better about it as Mom gave her a look.

"Come on, everybody. Let's make a toast to new beginnings."

Everybody took a few celebratory sips before preparing to return to their regular day. Rebecca said her good byes so she could head back to work.

Mom startled me from behind by poking me in my back.

"We're not the only ones looking forward to new beginnings. I saw you and Cole at the Luau. You look good together, you know."

"Oh, Mom. Don't get excited. We're just two friends going to grab a bite to eat."

"Really? You didn't mention anything about going to eat. That's what I call a date! When are you going?"

"I thought I mentioned it. We're going to The Cove this evening. He's supposed to pick me up around seven. I thought I'd head back over to the Inn for a few hours and then be back in time to get ready."

"You'll do no such thing. You'll take the rest the day off to pamper yourself and get ready for your special date."

"I have to get the maintenance orders in."

"Payton, you're not too old for me to put you over my knee."

"Okay, I surrender."

"What are you two over here making a fuss about?" William and Abby wanted in on the fun.

"Somebody has a date this evening with Cole Miller."

"Helen, didn't I tell you to stop meddling in their lives? They're grown women for goodness sake."

"Apparently, I'm not too grown for Mom to put me over her knee." I thought that was rather funny.

"I don't even want to know." He laughed at us and threw his hands in the air.

Dad made his way to his favorite recliner and left the ladies to talk amongst ourselves.

Abby offered to help me pick out an outfit for the evening.

"Are you excited about tonight?"

"I don't know how to feel, to be honest. I can clearly remember packing the car and leaving Connecticut just like it was yesterday. I don't know who I'm trying to kid by going out tonight. There's a part of me that wonders if this is all happening too soon."

"Payton, honestly, I think it's because you're putting a lot of mental pressure on yourself. You're overthinking the situation. Just go and have a good time. The least you'll get out of it is a good meal. Everybody needs to eat, right?"

Abby sifted through my closet, pulling out mostly new business clothes with tags.

"Okay, we may have a problem here. I either see business attire or yoga pants and sweats. What's wrong with this picture?"

"Before working at the Inn, I spent most of my days in casual wear."

"You and Jack never went out to dinner?"

"The first few years we did, but then the date nights stopped. Plus, I gained a little weight. All I really have is the Hawaiian dress that I wore the other night."

"No way. You're not wearing the same outfit. Come here. Let me look at you."

She twirled me around and sized me up.

"You don't look like you're more than 120 lbs soaking wet. Grab your bag. Clearly, we have a little shopping to do."

"Don't you have to get back to Wyatt and the kids?"

"I can head back as soon as we're done. Desperate times call for desperate measures."

"Oh, stop being such a drama queen."

"Hey! Be nice. This drama queen is going to make you look so good. Cole won't know what hit him."

I mumbled under my breath, "That's exactly what I'm afraid of."

"I heard that, Payton. Come on. Let's go."

"Coming."

The rest of the afternoon was spent shopping and treating myself to a mani-pedi.

"Yet another reason why I don't miss dating. All this pampering is for the birds."

I tried to patiently wait for my nails to dry. I was more into natural beauty than anything else. I figured as long as I kept my eyebrows shaped and a little color on my toes who cared about the rest? Shouldn't a man learn to like you just the way you are? Sweatpants and all. Somehow my philosophy always fell upon deaf ears among the women in the family.

Seven o'clock that evening rolled around rather quickly. I was sorry I didn't mention anything about eating earlier. My stomach usually started talking to me like clockwork every day around five. I popped one last cracker in my mouth while slipping into a pair of high heel sandals.

"Good Lord, help me walk in these things."

I swooshed mouthwash around my mouth a couple of times and proceeded to head downstairs.

"Cole. I didn't realize you were here already."

"Mrs. Matthews caught me outside, just as I was pulling up. You look stunning."

"Payton does clean up well, doesn't she?"

She stood admiring my transformation like a proud mom.

"Thanks, you look really nice."

"Well, get out there and have fun, you two. Cole, keep her out as late as you want. It's about time she learned how to have a little fun."

I widened my eyes at the remark, but my mother didn't pay me any mind.

"After you."

Cole was the perfect gentleman. I had butterflies in my stomach just being near him. He wore jeans and a sports jacket, which was the perfect outfit to match my fitted summer dress. If only I could manage to make it to the car without falling flat on my face. The last thing I needed was to wind up on the ground on our first date.

"Do you mind if I put the top down?"

"Not at all." Heck. If he didn't care about my hair looking like I was electrocuted, why should I?

"I may as well get this out of the way early... I hate dating," Cole said.

"So do I! I thought I was the only one."

"No. Not at all. It's so awkward when it's new. I'm that guy who likes to skip past anything weird and uncomfortable and get straight down to being relaxed. I just want to be my normal self."

"Minus all the nervousness, right?"

"Right. See, I knew you would understand. So let's make a pact."

"Okay."

"We're not doing the whole nervous thing."

"You will get no complaints out of me. Agreed!" I was darn near ready to change into my flats after that invitation. But I thought better of it for the moment.

"Good. Besides, we all know each other already. That puts me a step ahead of the rest."

"The rest?"

I looked around, pretending to figure out who the rest could be.

"I'm sure they're lining up at the door waiting to get your

name and number, Payton. If they aren't, give them just a little while longer to figure out you're back in town, and they will be."

He pulled into the parking lot at The Cove.

"This place looks nice."

"It does. Plus, it looks like we're going to have a beautiful sunset to enjoy from our table. Perfect night with the perfect lady."

Cole took me by the hand and let the valet park the car.

"There's only one thing needed to make the night complete."

"What's that?"

"Do you have a pair of flat shoes in your purse?"

Can you say Godsend? Who is this man, and why did it take me so long to meet him?

"Cole Miller, you know me a lot better than I thought."

"I was just thinking you might be a lot more comfortable if you weren't trying to walk around on stilts."

"Are you sure?"

"Yes, I'm sure. Payton, look at me. I think you're beautiful just the way you are."

His words were like music to my ears. I reached in my bag and pulled out a pair of flat sandals that I was saving for the end of the evening.

"Thank you, Cole. You just made me the happiest woman on the planet. I'm starting to wonder if you've been learning secrets about me from my mother."

"If that's all I had to do to make you happy, then you're pretty easy to please. As for the shoes, past experience has definitely been a teacher. I used to be married, remember?"

We were seated outdoors with a romantic view of the sunset and the water.

"How long were you married? If you don't mind me asking."

"Not at all. I was married for seven years. Laura passed away when Emmie was just three years old."

"Wow, that breaks my heart."

"It was a difficult time. She had a rare form of cancer that spread with a vengeance. Emmie was way too young to remember or understand what was going on. Before that time, we had a great marriage. We were both getting established in our careers and had big dreams together. Unfortunately, we never had a chance to pursue our dreams. Except for having Emmie, of course."

"She seems like such a sweet girl."

"I'm probably bias as her father, but I think so. She has a big heart, like her mother. She looks after her grandmother and me just as much as we look after her."

"Aww. She'd probably be a great role model for my niece Maggie and her brother. They're a bit younger then Emmie, but Maggie longs to have a girl to play with. She begs her mom for a sister all the time."

"Emmie would welcome her with open arms. We should get them all together sometime."

"That would be nice."

"If you don't mind me asking, how long were you married?"

"We barely made it to year five before things finally fell apart."

"Wow, that was a short-lived marriage."

"It's funny you should say that because, to me, it felt like an eternity."

"What happened?"

"You sure you want to know? We might be here for a while."

"I'm not in a hurry, but I don't want you to feel pressured if you don't want to talk about it."

"I'm an open book. Besides, I find talking about it to be

rather therapeutic. When I met Jack, he seemed to be in love with the idea of settling down and getting married. He even talked about how many kids he wanted. On and on, he would go, and I believed every word of it. About a year or so after we were married, we had trouble getting pregnant. We went to see a fertility specialist and tried everything possible, but nothing ever came of it. It was right around that time that I noticed he started growing distant. His work hours grew longer and slowly, but surely we became more like housemates rather than husband and wife. I felt ashamed when I finally learned of his affairs. The writing was on the wall, but I didn't want to accept it. I forgave him the first time thinking if he was sincere, we could heal from it and move on. The second time, not only did he cheat again, but he served me with divorce papers. I thought surely he believed he found "the one." My heart was torn to pieces, but I signed on the dotted line and gave him his freedom."

"You gained your freedom from the dirtbag. That's what matters most."

"Yeah, I guess that's a good way to look at it. The only problem is since then he's made a couple of appearances. I don't know if it's remorse or what. The whole thing is just crazy. But I'm glad it's finally behind me."

"Me too. I'm sorry you had to go through that."

"That makes two of us. I'd like to believe that it's making me stronger. Besides, now I'm back here with the family, and I have a bright future ahead of me. I wouldn't trade that for anything."

"Speaking of your bright future, I have a surprise for you. By any chance, are you free to take a quick little ride on Saturday morning?"

"I can be. Surely you're not going to keep the surprise a secret all the way until Saturday, are you?"

"Sorry, I have to. I'm sworn to secrecy, what can I say?"

I swatted my napkin playfully at Cole.

"That's not fair."

"I know, but trust me. It will be worth it."

"It better be." I teased.

"I'm not very good with surprises. I should warn you in advance that I have a strong tendency to ask at least a thousand and one questions until I figure out what it is."

"A thousand and one? Really. Well, thanks for the heads up. You can ask as many questions as you like, but I'm not going to budge."

"We'll see about that."

We finished our meal and talked for hours that evening. It was amazing how much life had turned a corner for me. No more late nights waiting for my husband to come home, or tears and sleepless nights. Instead, a date with a man who seemed to be everything I've ever dreamed of. That didn't mean I didn't have questions still lingering in the back of my mind. Was I really ready to date again? Perhaps this was too good to be true.

PAYTON

The usual Saturday morning breakfast was canceled due to everyone's busy schedule. It worked out perfectly for my morning date with Cole. Getting ready didn't take nearly as long as I put on my favorite yoga pants, racerback tee, and lipgloss. I tied my hair in a ponytail, but didn't throw all caution to the wind when it came to appearance. The look I was going for was effortless beauty. If mom were home, she would totally scold me for it.

"So, you're still not going to give me a hint?"

Cole closed my passenger door and made his way to the other side.

"Come on; you've made it this long. Just another five minutes won't kill ya."

"I guess you're right. I just can't hardly imagine what kind of surprise you could have up your sleeve."

"I found something pretty fascinating, and I thought you'd like it too."

"Hmm. Well, the suspense is killing me, so let's change the subject until we get there."

"That's more like it."

"Where's Emmie this morning?"

"She's at the house with my mom. We have a special daddy, daughter date planned for later on."

"That should be fun."

"Before I left, she managed to convince her grandmother to bake a cake. A cake with lots of chocolate icing were her precise words."

"I'll bet she didn't have to do much convincing. Grandparents have a way of giving in easily."

"Oh, you bet. By the time I get home, she'll be on a sugar high."

I enjoyed hearing the way Cole talked about his daughter.

"Do you think you would ever want more children if you remarried?"

"I always thought about how nice it would be for Emmie to have a little brother or sister. But I'm also in my forties now so..."

"It's not impossible to have more kids in your forties."

"I know. I'm open. Just more realistic if that makes sense."

"It does."

"Do you know what else I'm realistic about?"

"What?"

"The fact that it's time to close your eyes. No peeking allowed."

"Are you serious?"

"Yes, Ma'am. Come on. Eyes shut."

"Okay. I'm going out on a limb and trusting you, Cole Miller."

"Don't worry. You're in good hands."

Cole stopped the car and made his way around to lead me by the hand. I could tell we were in the heart of town in Pelican Beach by the sound of the church bells ringing.

"Okay, I want you to stop right there."

"This is so exciting!"

"Before you open your eyes clearly, you heard the church bells, so you may have a little inkling about what street we're on, but you still don't know exactly where we are."

The suspense was driving me crazy.

"Alright. On the count of three open your eyes. One... two... three..."

I opened my eyes to the site of an old white house nestled among other retail shops. It had an inviting front porch with a sign in the window that said retail space for rent.

"What do you think?"

"Well, it's nice. But I don't get what you want me to see."

"Take a closer look. It's your vision. It may not be exactly as you saw it in your mind, but it has great potential. Come here."

He took me by the hand and led me up to the front porch.

"It's an older house built in the 1940s. Not quite the 20's but still. I looked up an old listing online, and the 40's still gives it that older feel. If you look in the front window, it's set up parlor-style with lots of display shelves for your photo albums."

I peered inside the front window. One thing's for sure, Cole was definitely a good listener.

"I spoke to the owners, and they said the place used to be a retail shop for jewelers. And, look, before I go any further, I know you're dedicated to helping your parents out at the Inn right now. I just wanted to show you that your dream exists right here in Pelican Beach. If it's not this place, then some other retail spot, but whenever you're ready, your dream awaits you."

I could feel my eyes tearing up.

"Cole. This is amazing. Thank you. No one has ever done anything like this for me before."

"It's not a big deal. I just remember what it was like when I wanted to launch the renovation company. I had so many ideas and dreams, yet it felt like I had just as many obstacles in the way. If it wasn't for having the right people by my side to cheer me on, I might not be where I am today.

"It may not be today, but don't give up. You can do this."

"I'm speechless. I mean... your timing is impeccable. So much has changed for me within the last couple of days. I don't know. Maybe this is something I can look into soon."

"Is everything okay?"

"Yes, yes. Oh my gosh. I don't mean to imply anything bad. I was going to mention it to you, but my parents have decided to sell."

"The cottage or the Inn?"

"The Inn."

"Wow. I can't imagine anyone else running that place."

"Neither can I."

We sat down on the porch swing to talk.

"I was going to mention it to you because we had the best intentions of having you back for renovations. However, when they sat us down and talked about my dad's health, and their desire to lift the pressure off, it made a lot of sense."

"I know it must be tough, but it's a wise decision."

"It is. As Dad would say, it's bittersweet."

"Before I forget, I'll be sure to have Martha draw a check to return your father's deposit."

"Thank you, Cole."

"It looks like this will give you a clean break to focus on what you want."

"I guess you're right. I haven't had a moment to think about it. The place that I wanted to rent fell through, and my parents will no longer need help at the Inn. It seems like I have so many options before me until I don't know what to do with myself these days."

It seemed stupid, but I had to laugh at myself to keep from crying.

"I guess I just need to be thankful that I'm not where I used to be."

"And thankful that you're one step closer to your future business."

"Yes. Thank you, Cole." I quickly dabbed the corner of my eyes to hide my pain and fears. Cole was right. I had so many options before me, yet I didn't know how to handle it. I was so used to my old life. The thought of embracing something this big was kind of scary.

"You can thank me by grabbing a quick bagel before we head back."

"Only if it's topped with cream cheese."

"One bagel and cream cheese coming right up. How about we make our way over to the little coffee shop across the street?"

"Sounds good. You heard my stomach growling, didn't you?"

"Nooo, not at all."

He looked at me from the corner of his eye and smiled.

"Hey, Payton."

"Yes?"

"I like you a lot. As if you couldn't already tell."

"That's so sweet."

"But..."

"I really think it's sweet. You're definitely not like any other guy I've ever met."

"Thanks for that, but I can still hear a hesitant sound in your voice."

"It has nothing to do with you. I think you're an amazing guy. You just happen to catch me at a time when I'm trying to figure things out."

"Ouch."

"Ouch?"

"Yep. It's the good ole, it's not you, it's me line."

"Cole."

"No, no. It's okay. I get it."

He held the door open for me. I was slowly starting to lose my appetite. What seemed like a lovely morning was slightly shifting as the conversation became uncomfortable.

"Hey, we agreed not to do awkward, remember?" I nudged him a bit.

"You're right. Plus, I don't want to be selfish. Just know that I think you're a gem. Women like you aren't easy to come by. I'm so sorry your ex-husband didn't value you. Even more so, I'm sorry that he ruined it for a guy like me. If you need more time, I get it. No pressure."

I appreciated Cole's support and believed he was sincere. However, I was too overtaken with fear to give in and admit my feelings for him.

The ride back was filled with general talk about our plans for the weekend. Before long, he dropped me off at my parents' house and thanked me for coming along for the ride. I walked around to his side of the car to say my final goodbyes.

"I'm the one who should be thanking you. Thank you for encouraging me, Cole. I meant it when I said no one has ever done anything like that for me."

He placed his hand over mine. "I meant it too. If you ever want to hang out again, you know how to find me."

I backed away from the car and watched him leave. On what should've been a wonderful start to the day somehow left me with nothing but feelings of sadness.

PAYTON

"*H*ow are you feeling, Dad?"

"I've had better days, Payton. Come in and sit with me for a while."

I stepped into his office and made myself comfortable on the couch.

"Is there something I can do to make you feel better?"

"No, not really. I think I just needed a break. I have to be honest and admit I've been pushing myself too hard this week. It's starting to catch up to me, that's all."

"Aww, Dad. I wish you wouldn't. It isn't worth it. Things should be getting easier at this point. Not worse. You and mom have a good offer on the Inn. I can't even imagine what you could be stressing over."

"I'm having a hard time letting go. Outside of raising you and your sisters, this place was our baby. It makes me sad to watch all of the guests come and go knowing that in just a short while, they will no longer be our guests."

"Do you regret your decision?"

"I still think it was the right thing to do. It's just difficult.

Besides, the old mind isn't stable anymore. It could never work even if I wanted to cancel the deal and stay."

"I don't care what the doctors say. In my eyes, there's nothing old or unstable about your mind."

"Thank you, Darlin. Promise me something, Payton."

"Yes?"

"When I'm at the point where it's difficult for me to do so, please take care of your mother for me."

"Dad, you know I will, but please don't talk like that."

"You know I'm a realist. But enough about me. It seems like you've been moping around this place all morning. Are you feeling alright?"

"I didn't realize it. I guess I just have a lot on my mind."

"I always tell your mother she shouldn't get in the middle of these sorts of things. If I had to guess, is it about a special someone that you've taken an interest in?"

The look on my face confirmed that he knew what he was talking about.

"You seemed rather happy the other day. What's bothering you?"

"I'm trying to figure out if I made the right decision. Cole expressed his feelings for me, but I told him it was bad timing because I was trying to figure things out."

"What exactly are you trying to figure out?"

"It's no secret why I moved back home. Now that the divorce is behind me, I've been trying to figure out how to move forward. I need to decide what I'm going to do about my career, I need to eventually find a place to live. I don't see how I could have time to focus on a new relationship when everything else is out of sorts."

"I thought your career path was a no brainer. We always knew your time at the Inn was temporary. You have dreams to pursue unless something changed that I'm not aware of. As for a place to stay, that's also easy. I know you probably want to have a place of your own. There's nothing wrong with that. But don't you think it would be easier to continue to stay at the cottage until your new business gets underway?"

"I guess. I didn't want to be a bother."

"Payton, no matter how old you get, you're our daughter. You're never a bother."

"Thanks, Dad."

"Now getting back to this special interest of yours. You said he goes by the name of Cole Miller, is that correct?"

"Yes, Sir. You're correct."

"Mmm-hmm. Well, don't tell your mother I said so, but she's right. He's a respectable young man. Cole and little Emmie would make a nice match for you. But more importantly, you have to stop being so hard on yourself. If I waited until every little thing was all figured out, I would've never married your mother, had children, or started a business for that matter."

"But what about the divorce? It hasn't been that long. Don't you think I'd be moving a little too fast?"

"I can't answer that question for you, but there is something you should consider. According to what you shared with us, your marriage was over long before you signed the papers. Not by your choice but by Jack's choosing. You tried to do everything you could to hold that marriage together. Even when most could've argued against it. Set yourself free, Payton. Move on."

"Wow. Guess I hadn't been looking at it that way, but you're right. I thought I left everything behind me the day I slammed the door in his face. But apparently, I was still holding on."

"Do you want to go back?"

"Heck, no!"

MICHELE GILCREST

"Then set yourself free to enjoy what the future has in store."

"Have I ever told you how much I love you, Dad?"

"Never hurts to hear it again."

"Aww, I love you. Thank you for your words of wisdom."

I sprang to my feet and gave dad a tight squeeze.

"There's that smile I like to see. Now go on and invite Cole and Emmie over for dinner."

"I'll think about it."

"Ok. When you're done thinking, be sure to give him a call."

I turned around and gave him a look before heading out the door. Dad chuckled, knowing it wasn't a matter of if I would do it, but when.

For the remainder of the day, I worked on room inventory. I worked with housekeeping to make sure the rooms were fully supplied and filled out order forms for anything that needed to be replaced. I walked through the rooms with a view of the garden, and then those with the ocean view. When all of a sudden, an idea came to mind.

"Hey Abby, it's Payton. Do you have a few minutes to talk?"

"Sure, what's up?"

"I'm at the Inn, sitting in one of our suites that overlook the water."

"Okayyy."

"Well, an idea came to mind about having a last hoorah for the ladies before we sell the Inn."

"I'm listening."

"What if we blocked off one of the suites with adjoining rooms for an overnight stay? It could be me, you, Mom, Becca, and maybe even a couple of friends."

"Sounds like fun as long as your other sister can behave herself."

"Abby, come on, be serious."

"I am being serious."

I sat silent for a moment to let her know I didn't like the negative sister talk.

"Alright. I'll stop talking about her."

"Thank you. She is your sister too, you know. Besides, she was right the other day. It's time to grow up."

"I'll stop, Payton. Now go on with your idea."

"Okay. So we could make a full day of it, including breakfast the next morning, and hanging out at the beach. We can be more like guests and make it a girls sleepover. What do you think?"

"I'm game. Why don't you rally up the troops and we can all confirm a day that works best."

"Yes! I figured you would be in. I'll arrange things with Mom and Becca and see if everybody wants to do just us girls or invite a few others."

"I'm in either way. Thanks Payton, great idea!"

"Awesome. Well, I have to get back to inventory. Give a hug to my precious niece and nephew."

"Will do."

"Bye."

I hung up, feeling pretty excited about the idea. I knew it wouldn't be hard to convince the others to get on board. There was only one other piece of business that was lingering in my mind and needed to be settled. I decided to work up the nerve and send a text message to Cole.

Payton: Hey, Cole. How are you?

I waited a few minutes before returning to work. I was determined not to be disappointed if he decided not to respond.

Cole: Hi, Payton. Sorry for the delay. I was in a meeting. I'm well. How are you?

Payton: I'm great. Sorry to bother you. I'm sure you're pretty busy.

Cole: You're not bothering me. I'm happy to hear from you.

Payton: Good to know. I was hoping we could get together soon and talk?

Cole: It's just Emmie and me tonight, so I can't really get away.

Payton: No problem. I understand.

Cole: Not so fast. If you're willing to stop by, we can talk on the porch after she goes to bed.

Payton: Sure.

Cole: Free around eight o'clock?

Payton: Eight o'clock works.

Cole: Great. I'll send you my address.

Payton: Sounds good.

Precisely at eight o'clock, I pulled up to Cole's house. The view was absolutely amazing. His house was ideally situated with a view of the beach from his back porch. I made my way around to the back, as instructed in his text.

"Wow, now I see why you like to hang out on the porch. This is absolutely breathtaking."

"Thank you."

"Gosh, the little rental I was looking at is small-time compared to this place."

"Trust me when I tell you that I'm very humbled at the opportunity to live here. Please have a seat."

We joined each other on the swing set.

"It was truly a matter of perfect timing that allowed me to get this place. I was working on a renovation a few doors down when I heard this house was under foreclosure. The asking price was very low because it needed a lot of work."

"Ahh. Of course, it all makes sense. This is your field of expertise."

"Correct. Emmie and I were actually living closer to my mother at the time. I thought buying this place was also an opportunity to put her in better schools. Living on the beach was a bonus. In a lot of ways, it was a fresh start for both of us."

"Well, from what I can tell, you did a phenomenal job. I can't tell this place was ever a fixer-upper."

"Thank you. I'm thankful for the resources to get the place up to speed."

"I'm sure your skills have come in handy on many occasions."

"These hands have served me well, and I'm definitely humbled and thankful. But enough about me. Can I offer you a drink?"

"I'm good, thank you. I didn't plan to stay long. I know you have to look after Emmie."

"No worries. She's upstairs in bed. My girl likes to play hard during the day and sleeps hard at night."

"I'll bet. Enjoy it now. I'm told that all changes when they become teenagers."

"I'm sure it does. Even we can remember what the teenage years were like. I used to shut off the lights and pretend like I was going to bed but sneak my walkman and listen to my favorite music."

"Oh man, I haven't heard someone mention a walkman in ages. Those were the good old days. Back when cassette tapes were in style."

"What do you know about cassette tapes?"

"Umm, hello. I still have a box full saved in storage. I'll bet I can find my walkman and my boombox if I look hard enough."

"See, I knew I liked you."

Laughing and sharing old memories came easily with Cole.

I knew I would have to find the nerve to share why I texted him in the first place. The fun-loving banter subsided, and we grew quiet.

"Cole?"

"Yes."

"About earlier, when I texted you."

"Yes."

"I've been thinking. Perhaps I've been letting fear get in the way. The last time we were together, you told me you liked me. The truth is I like you too."

Cole took me by the hand while he continued looking out to the ocean.

"So perhaps we just need to take this thing slowly."

"I'd like that."

"I'm glad you reached out to me today. There's nothing I wanted more than for you to change your mind."

"Really? I thought surely you had written me off after the other day."

"Never. How could I write off someone like you?"

He leaned over and traced my forehead, my cheeks, and my lips with his fingers.

That evening we continued to enjoy the newness of our affection for one another. I was finally starting to embrace a new season in my life, one that would hopefully propel me forward into a loving relationship with Cole.

PAYTON

*E*arly Friday morning, I received a message from Cole. Anytime I saw his name show up on my phone was a welcomed treat, so today would be no exception.

"Nancy, I'll be out by the pool, returning a phone call in case anybody is looking for me."

"Okay. Don't forget about your eleven o'clock appointment. The new owner Mr. Thompson had his secretary call to confirm his visit today."

"Yes, eleven o'clock. I'm on it. Be sure to remind my mom for me."

"I'll call her now."

I strolled over to the poolside while checking my voicemail from Cole.

"Hi, Payton. It's me, Cole. Please call me when you get a chance. I have a major favor to ask you."

Curious to know what his message could be about, I gave him a call.

"Hello?"

"Hi, Cole. What's up?"

"Oh, Payton. So glad to hear your voice."

"I heard your message. You sounded like something was wrong. Is everything okay?"

"Everything is fine. It's just, we have a little bit of a family emergency. My cousin Christen is getting married in Naples tomorrow. Unfortunately, her photographer had to back out on her due to a death in the family. As you can imagine, she's desperate to find a replacement, and I was wondering if, by any chance, you would be free to help her out?"

"Tomorrow? My gosh, Cole. I just recovered my equipment from storage this week, but I haven't even unpacked everything yet. Plus, preparing for a wedding photo shoot is a big deal. I would need to restock on my film, and test the equipment. I don't know, Cole."

"Please, Payton? You would be doing us a huge favor. Plus, it would be great exposure for your business. I know she will have a lot of guests from the area who would love to hire you. Word of mouth spreads quickly. I told her about you. She's willing to pay double if you can help her out."

"I can't believe I'm saying this, but I'll do it."

"Yes! Thank you so much."

"This would be a good opportunity for me to get my feet wet again. As long as she understands that I don't run a big operation and I may be a bit rusty at first."

"Stop being so hard on yourself. I've seen some of your photos at the cottage. You know exactly what you're doing."

"Well, I'm still nervous. This is your family. The pressure is on big time."

"Everybody is going to love you, Payton. You're a professional. You got this!"

"You just better be lucky I like you, Cole Miller."

"I consider myself to be lucky every day."

It felt so dreamy to hear him talk like that I almost had to pinch myself. I loved the way he placed so much confidence in my abilities and the way he believed in me.

"Where is she getting married?"

"At the Marina Clubhouse in Naples. It's right on North Beach."

"Wow, swanky."

"That's Christen and Jacob for you."

"Okay, text me her number, and I'll give her a call. I have to wrap up an important meeting here at the Inn, then I can shift gears and focus on the wedding."

"Thanks again, Payton. I owe you big time. Hey, one more thing before you go."

"Yes?"

"When you're not taking pictures, maybe I can steal a dance or two?"

"I think we can make that happen."

"Okay, I'll talk to you soon."

"Bye."

I ended the call, not knowing whether to be nervous or excited. However, I had to tuck the nerves away for a bit and head to my mother's office. Today we were meeting with our buyer to help him get acquainted with the Inn.

"Mr. Thompson, welcome. It's nice to have you."

"Please call me David. I'm grateful for this rare opportunity."

"Allow me to introduce you to my daughter, Payton. She's been helping us run things here at the Inn, and I thought it might be helpful to have her sit in on the meeting."

I extended my hand to try and make him feel welcomed.

"It's so nice to meet you."

He seemed to be a little flirtatious as he introduced himself, but I chose to ignore it. Mom diverted his attention back to the purpose of their meeting.

"My husband sent his regards and apologized for not being able to make it today. He's feeling a bit under the weather."

"I understand."

Everyone took a seat around her table to talk further.

"David, I know you had a chance to have a formal inspection already. Over the next couple of weeks, it's really just down to the agents tying up loose ends. We thought you might be interested in taking a personal tour of the facility and perhaps even meet the staff."

"Helen, that's kind of you, but I don't think it will be necessary. You know how it is. New ownership usually comes with new ideas and likely new staff."

I saw the look of shock in my mother's eyes. Mr. Thompson wasn't necessarily wrong, but he didn't have to be so crude about it.

"Well, then. If you don't mind me asking, how can we help you today?"

"I came here to see if we could speed things up. Time is ticking, and I'd like to get some renovations underway so I can turn this place into a gold mine. I figure if you put in a simple call, surely we can bump things up to next week. If it's just a matter of some paperwork, I'm sure I can offer the real estate team a little something to motivate them. If you know what I mean."

The look on his face was one of arrogance. I could tell he was impressed with himself.

"Mom, please allow me to share a few thoughts."

She gave me a nod of approval. It was all I could do not to haul off and give him a piece of my mind.

"Mr. Thompson, I'm sure I speak on behalf of both of my parents when I say that we won't be able to accommodate you. We plan on giving our staff the proper time needed to prepare for this transition. Before you leave, I'd like to offer you a piece of advice. One of the reasons the Inn at Pelican Beach has become such a successful destination for many to enjoy is because we're so much more than your average name-brand hotel. We also place a major emphasis on community. It takes a special someone to be able to blend the two together and deliver in a way that's well-received. Just something for you to think about. Is there anything else we can assist you with today?"

"No. Not at all. If you change your mind about turning over the keys earlier, you have my number. If not, I'll see you at our regularly scheduled closing. Thank you for your time."

"Allow me to escort you out."

He didn't say anything further. Just as well because I didn't care to hear it anyway. I led the way to the main lobby.

"I guess I'll be seeing you in a couple of weeks, Miss Matthews. You take care."

"Likewise."

I returned to the office, fuming over his arrogance. Mom didn't appear to be too pleased either by the look on her face.

"Thank you for handling that, Dear."

"It was my pleasure. Can you believe the nerve of that guy?"

"I don't know what's gotten into people these days. Honestly, there was nothing wrong with him asking to advance things along. It was just his approach and clear disregard for the staff."

"I hear about situations like this all the time. Some big wig comes in town and cares about nothing else but the money. If you agree, I think we should give everyone a heads up."

"You're right. We won't alarm them, but just let them know he may have plans of his own."

"Okay. In the meantime, I'm glad we have these last couple of weeks to celebrate. This place has always been more like a home away from home rather than work. We're all one big family here."

"Yes, it's just like your father says. It's bittersweet."

"I'm also grateful for the extra time I'll have to take care of him. Some days he really worries me, Payton. This morning he repeated the same question on three different occasions. Other days he's like his old self."

"I know, Mom. We're all here for you guys. You do know that, right?"

"Yes, Honey, we do. Onto something more uplifting. How are things going with you and Cole?"

"Pretty good. Speaking of Cole, I promised to do the photography for his cousin's wedding tomorrow."

"That's wonderful. I don't remember you saying anything about a wedding."

"I just accepted the job today. She was in desperate need of someone because her photographer canceled."

"Poor thing. She must've been frantic. I'm sure you made her day by taking the job."

"Yes, but if I'm going to pull this thing off, I need to get going. I have a few stops to make, and I then I have to get back to the house to test the cameras."

"Well, run along. We're fine here. I'll hold down the fort."

"You sure, Mom?"

"I'm certain."

I was so grateful, I kissed her and hurried along to get everything I needed for the wedding.

The next day I arrived at the venue early to set up for the ceremony. The clubhouse was set just a few feet away from North Beach shores with the most romantic view of the ocean. Inside I snapped a few shots of the arch where the couple would exchange their vows. It was decorated with chiffon

THE INN AT PELICAN BEACH

draping and gorgeous flowers. I paused to take in the beauty of the space when I felt a tap on the shoulder.

"Hello, beautiful."

The voice was instantly recognized. When I turned around, Cole's handsome smile made my heart flutter.

"Cole. Look at you."

"I hope that's a good thing."

"It is. You look so handsome."

"Thank you, but you're the one who's taking my breath away."

He placed a strand of my hair back in place then softly kissed me on the forehead.

"Looks like you've been busy already."

"Yes, but there's still lots to do. I need to make my way to the bridal suite to get a few shots of the ladies getting ready. Your sweet distractions are going to make me late. I'll see you in a bit?"

"I'm looking forward to it. Oh, before I forget. My mom and Emmie are here. I'd love for you to come say hello later when you have time."

I didn't want to get my lipstick on him, so I teased him with a little nose rub.

"I can't wait."

"Alright. Go get 'em, tiger."

There was something about Cole that was gentle and kind and so familiar. This wedding was giving me so much more than the opportunity to use my camera again. Cole was helping me make room in my heart to love again.

After I wrapped up with the ladies upstairs, I had a brief moment to chat with the bride.

"Thank you so much for helping me out. You don't know how much this means. I could never repay you."

"I'm happy I was able to help. You look absolutely stunning."

"Thank you. Please make sure you make time to enjoy yourself in between taking pictures."

She began to whisper, not wanting anyone to hear.

"The word among the family is Cole really likes you. He hasn't talked about a special someone in his life since his wife passed away. I know I'm biased as his cousin, but he's a really great guy."

I couldn't hold back my smile. Her words felt so good to hear.

"Oh, that smile of yours says a mouthful. You get him, girl!"

"Thank you, Christen. In the meantime, I'm going to snap a few pictures of your husband to be. I'll see you in a little while."

"Okay!" She was so excited to be marrying the man of her dreams.

I turned back one last time.

"Christen."

"Yes."

"Thanks for the advice."

"Anytime!"

I walked past the glass windows with the view of the beach and some early guests starting to arrive. I was inspired and had visions of my photography business getting underway soon. Tonight love was in the air, and I planned to explore everything love had to offer.

Once the reception was well underway, I made my way over to Cole's table.

"Hi, Miss Payton."

"Hi, Emmie. How's the wedding cake?"

"Delicious. I'm on my second piece. Would you like to try some?"

"Why, thank you. I will have a piece."

"Emmie, I think we better slow down with the cake before you find yourself with a tummy ache," Cole interjected.

"Just one last bite, please, Dad?"

"One last bite, and then you're done, kiddo."

"Okay."

"Payton, you remember my mother from the Luau?"

"Yes, Mrs. Miller, it's so good to see you."

"It's good to see you too, Payton. I can see why Cole is so fond of you." She nudged Cole on the arm.

"You look gorgeous."

"Thank you for the compliment, Mrs. Miller."

"Please call me, Alice."

I found a blush pink maxi dress on sale that complimented my figure. With a little make-up and my hair in a bun, I figured it was the perfect way to blend in with the guests.

"Hey Mom, I thought you were on my team. You can't be giving away all my secrets." Cole teased.

"Trust me, Son, I didn't say anything Payton doesn't already know."

Emmie looked at her dad with a grin.

"Thank you, Alice. I'm afraid my coming over here may have started something."

"Aww, it's all in fun. Have you two had a chance to dance yet?"

"No, we haven't. I've been busy taking pictures most of the evening."

"Well, Cole. It looks to me like your dancing partner awaits you."

Cole stood up and extended his hand to me.

"Would you like to join me on the dance floor?"

"Absolutely."

I followed Cole as he led me to the dance floor. I didn't know the name of the song playing, but it didn't matter. I felt like no one else was in the room except for Cole and me as we danced in each other's arms.

"This is the highlight of my night," Cole said.

"Mine too. I can't think of the last time I danced."

"That makes two of us. Now I know what to plan for our next date night."

"Good luck getting this girl to keep up at a night club."

"Who said anything about a night club? We can have our own private dance party right in my backyard."

"Now we're talking. That kind of date is definitely more my speed."

He spun me around and wrapped his arms around me from behind.

"Look at you with the fancy moves."

"Haha, that's as fancy as it gets. As soon as they speed the music up here come the two left feet."

"Aww."

Back at the table, I could hear Emmie just a couple of feet away saying, "Look at daddy dancing."

Then an older and distinguished looking woman joined Alice at the table. She spoke rather loudly over the music.

"Alice, it's been a while. How are you?"

"Carol Donovan, I'm wonderful. Don't you look fabulous? How have you been?"

"Too busy for my own good. Charles tells me all the time that I need to slow down. Eventually, I'll listen. Besides, my daughter Lexi is still working with me at the boutique, so that helps."

"Oh, that's nice."

"Yes."

Carol looked over and watched Cole and I as we danced.

"Alice, I know it's been a little while since I've seen Cole, but is everything ok?"

"It couldn't be better. What makes you ask?"

"Well, I see him over there dancing with the help. Poor guy. He must be lonely not having anyone in his life since Laura's passing."

Did she just call me the help? Surely I was hearing wrong.

"The help? Oh, that's Payton Matthews. She's the daughter of William and Helen Matthews, who own The Inn at Pelican Beach."

"Really? I didn't know."

"Yes, she's doing us all a huge favor tonight. Christen's photographer couldn't make it. And since she's a professional photographer, she stepped in to help."

"Interesting. I don't think I've seen her around before."

"She hasn't been back too long. She was living in Connecticut until she got a divorce. Now she's helping her folks out at the Inn. Cole says she's a very talented photographer. I think she plans on opening up a business at some point."

"A divorcee, hmm. I always thought my Lexie would make a fine match for someone like Cole. He needs a certain caliber of a woman by his side. You know, someone who will represent his name and his business well in the community. A classy lady without baggage."

Surely this woman didn't realize I could hear every word she was saying. I decided to continue enjoying the dance with Cole and ignore it. Besides, it would be foolish of me to think other women didn't want to be with Cole.

Both women sat and watched us on the dance floor.

"Payton really is lovely, Carol. I'm sure you would think the same if you knew her."

"Oh well. Maybe I can get to know her sooner than we think. I could use some photos of my new collection for my website. You should give me her contact information."

"Certainly. I'll ask her for a business card tonight. Or better yet, I can just text her number to your phone."

"Lovely. Well, Alice, it's been nice seeing you as always. I'm going to make my rounds and say hello to a few more people."

"It was good seeing you."

The woman appeared to be giving her a kiss on both cheeks before making her way to the next table.

"Sounds like my mother is over there recruiting some business for you," Cole said.

"That's nice of her. Referrals can go a long way for small businesses."

"Tell me about it."

"But the lady she was talking to didn't seem too fond of me."

"Don't take it that way. She has a way about poking her nose around where it isn't warranted but the Donovans are genuinely good people."

Cole continued to lead for the final moments of the song.

"Payton Matthews, I'm falling for you," he whispered.

Words couldn't describe the way he made me feel. I had come a long way from being married to someone who didn't love me the way I deserved to be loved.

HELEN

*T*he following weekend all of us were getting together at the Inn for our last hoorah. Our Saturday morning breakfast had an entirely new meaning, as this would be the last time we'd gather together at the Inn. I started my usual questioning and making sure everything was in order.

"Payton, are you ready? We're going to be late, Dear."

"Coming Mom, just grabbing my camera."

"What a wonderful idea."

"Yeah, I was thinking we can capture a few memories and maybe even frame a few pictures for everyone."

"Marvelous. You know how much I love hanging pictures around the house."

"Do you have everything?"

"I think so. If not, it's not like we're far from the house. Let me just check on your father and Wyatt to make sure they're all set."

We were all packed and ready for a fun overnight stay at the Inn, while Wyatt was going to stay back and keep William and the kids company.

You could tell Will didn't approve of all the extra attention.

"Helen, you girls go and have a good time. Don't worry about me, Wyatt, or the grandkids. We have plenty of things to do to keep us occupied."

"That's what I'm afraid of. Wyatt, I'm counting on you to make sure William is in one piece when I get back."

"Yes, Ma'am, don't you worry. I'm on it."

Abby was more concerned about the house being in shambles.

"Yes, keep Dad in one piece, and please keep the kids from turning the house upside down," Abby said.

"Babe, don't worry. We have everything under control. It's only one evening. Go and have a good time."

I agreed with Wyatt. "He's right, it's only one evening. Let's go have some fun, girls!"

Payton, Abby, and I drove over to the Inn to meet Rebecca. Their long time friend, Susan, would be stopping by for a little while as well.

When we arrived at the suite, Rebecca had a tray of Mimosas ready for everyone.

"Now that we're all here. This is going to be so fun," Rebecca said.

Payton hugged Susan. She hadn't seen her since the wedding. They all grew up in the same neighborhood together. Susan was there for all of the significant milestones, so today wouldn't be any different.

"Susan, it's been a while. I'm glad you could make it to celebrate with us."

"So am I. Come here and give me a hug."

Rebecca took it upon herself to get the festivities started. "Okay, before everybody starts getting sappy, we need to grab a glass and make a toast."

Everyone followed suit and gathered around Rebecca.

"To Mom, Dad, and all of the wonderful memories created here at the Inn. More importantly, to all that lies ahead. Cheers."

"Cheers!" Everyone tapped glasses and took their first sip.

"I don't know about you ladies, but our Saturday morning tradition calls for some breakfast. Let's head downstairs to the veranda and then make our way to the beach." I knew I wouldn't be the only one who was hungry.

"Just what the doctor ordered. Food!" Payton agreed but she wasn't one for much drinking anyway.

Everything was set up for us downstairs by the staff in our own private section of the Inn. We had a table for five overlooking the gorgeous array of flowers that lined the veranda.

I kicked off the conversation as we all sat down. "You know, I think this is the first time I've really enjoyed the Inn as a guest. This really is such a nice treat."

"I hope the next owner does us proud," Abby said.

Payton and I glanced at each other.

"Don't hold your breath with that one, Abby."

"What makes you say that?"

"Payton and I had a chance to meet with him the other day. He seemed to be in a big hurry to get in. He wanted to push up the closing date and had a lot of ideas for a complete overhaul."

Payton nodded in agreement. "Mom's right. He seems more of the big chain type. I'm not so sure he has a good understanding of what the Inn experience is all about."

Susan chimed in. "I don't know how well that's going to go over here in Pelican Beach. People have come to expect a certain standard of luxury accommodations, of course, but that's not the only thing that makes this place tick. It's the personalized touch, and the sense of community that really brings it all together. The guests comment about it all the time. It would be a shame to lose that."

I adamantly agreed. "Exactly, Susan. I'm fearful he doesn't get that at all. But what can I do? Absolutely nothing. He has the right as the new owner to do whatever he wants to do."

"Don't you worry, Mrs. Matthews. When he starts losing business, he'll be forced to figure it out. Tourists aren't the only ones that like to come to the Inn. The locals help keep this place afloat as well," Susan said.

"No matter what he decides to do, we're not going to let it spoil the bond we have with the people of Pelican Beach. Furthermore, we're not going to let it ruin our special day," Rebecca said.

My daughter meant well but that must've been the Mimosas kicking in. I can't recall the last time she had much interest in anything other than having a good time.

Later that morning, the ladies and I laid out on the beach and indulged in a little girl talk. Susan asked to hear all the details about Payton's new beau.

"So what's this I hear about a new beau, Payton?"

"Ha, one of my lovely sisters must've filled you in if you've heard something already."

They denied any wrongdoing.

"Mom? Was it you?"

"I don't know what you could possibly be talking about."

"Mmm, hmm. Sure, you don't. Well, I guess it's no secret anyway. We've been spending a lot of time together lately."

"We, meaning you and Cole Miller?" Susan said.

"Yes, do you know him?"

"Do I know him? He has the most popular renovation company in all of Pelican Beach, and he's hot. Do you know how many women would love to be in your shoes right now?"

"Out here? Not many, I would assume. Aren't most of the women out here married with kids?"

"Most, but not all."

"Yeah, Payton. We're not all married." Rebecca spoke on behalf of all the single women in town.

"Well, perhaps there are a few exceptions. He's so quiet and laid back. I don't even think he knows how much of a hot item he is. Or at least if he does, he never seems to show it, which I love," said Payton.

Susan questioned Payton a bit further. "Does it feel kind of strange being back out there dating again?"

"Not really. I guess I don't consider myself to be back out there. Things took an ugly nosedive with Jack. After that was over, I had absolutely no interest in seeing anyone. I just wanted to come back to Pelican and focus on getting my life in order. Meeting Cole was more like a sweet surprise. Very much unexpected."

I was happy it turned out that way. "That's usually how love shows up. In the most unexpected ways."

"I'm happy for you, Payton," Susan said.

"Thanks, Susan. How's everything with you, Ross, and the kids?"

"Pretty good. The kids are keeping me on my toes with all of their clubs and activities. I don't recall being nearly as busy when I was a child growing up. Ross and I have to be more intentional about penciling in date nights. We love our little ones, but if we're not careful, we can quickly find ourselves running low on adult time."

"I hear ya."

Payton sat up and reached in her bag for her camera. She took a couple of shots of the beach, she captured a sandcastle left behind by kids, and one or two shots of the Inn.

"This would make a nice brochure for a hotel or travel agency."

"Payton, when do you plan to get started on your business?" Susan said.

"Very soon. I found a renewed sense of passion after taking photos for the wedding. I'm definitely ready to dive back in and start building my client list."

I was pleased to hear that Payton was now going to start focusing on her dreams.

"Alright, get together, everyone. Let's get a group shot," Payton said.

"Oh, no, you don't. No candid photos of me showing all the weight I've gained. Let me put my sarong on." I was the more modest one of the group. The rest of them put on their beach hats, puckered their lips, and posed for the camera.

Then Susan diverted her attention to Abby. "So Abby, I see you and Wyatt are still going strong after everything. I'm happy to see you guys are doing okay."

"I'm not quite sure what you mean, Susan."

"You know, the whole thing with the legal assistant."

"I don't know what you're talking about. What whole thing?"

Susan had everyone's full attention at this point. As the older and wiser one of the group, my internal antennas started to rise. Something about this conversation was heading in the wrong direction.

"Never-mind. I'm sure I heard wrong," Susan said.

I noticed Rebecca appeared to be particularly amused by the look on Abby's face. As if we didn't already have a talk about how to treat your sisters. My motherly instinct made me want to snatch the smirk off her face.

Susan repeated herself. "I'm sure I made a mistake, Abby. Forget about it. You know how people are with gossip."

"Share, Susan. Clearly, you know something. You were confident enough to bring it up. What's the gossip all about?"

"I heard that one of the new legal assistants was coming on

real strong to Wyatt. There was something about the two of them having a fling. I just assumed you knew."

"Checkmate," Rebecca murmured.

I didn't have a problem stepping in and asking Rebecca to quit. And I felt even less remorse about giving Susan a piece of my mind.

"For the love of all things good, Rebecca, please hush your mouth. And Susan, I've heard just about enough of this. Surely you could've approached this differently? What has gotten into you?" In that moment I felt like a darn referee.

"No, Mom. Let her speak," Abby said. "Where did you hear such a thing?"

"Ross mentioned it, but again, Abby. It's all hearsay. I'm sorry. I made an assumption that you knew, and I was wrong."

"Anything else I need to know?"

"No. Abby, please. I'm sorry."

"Yeah. Listen, you guys go ahead and enjoy the rest of the day. I'm heading back to the house."

"Abby!" Payton pleaded, but it was no use. Clearly, Abby was angry.

Susan packed her things and left as well. Somehow what was supposed to be a fun day turned sour very quickly.

"Should we all just leave?" Payton asked.

I knew now more than ever Abby needed her space. "No, we need to stay right here. The last thing Abby needs is an audience when she gets back to the house," I said.

"And Rebecca, I don't know what's gotten into you lately, but whatever it is, you need to fix it fast. Abby is your sister, not your enemy. Half the things you two bicker over isn't worth the time of day. But today, you crossed the line."

"I'll apologize to her, Mom."

"Good."

PAYTON

$\mathcal{W}$e planned a nice afternoon to host the Millers at my parents' house. I was on pins and needles as it was our first time having everyone under the same roof. My parents went out of their way to make sure we had everything, and Abby brought the kids over to entertain Emmie.

"Sooo, this is a big day, how do you feel about Cole bringing his family over?" Abby asked.

"I'm excited. For some reason, I'm a little nervous as well."

"Why? There's no need to be nervous. You know, Mom and Dad adore Cole. Plus, it's not like you're in high school where you have to worry about your parents' approval."

"I know, but I still want everything to go smoothly. What if we run out of things to talk about? Or what if Emmie doesn't have a good time?"

"Payton, stop. You're being ridiculous."

"I know, but sometimes things start to change when a relationship gets serious."

"Now we're getting down to the good stuff! So you consider yourselves to be serious?"

"I mean, he is coming over here to spend time with the family, Abby. I don't want to blow things out of proportion, but we've definitely been more exclusive lately. Cole is just an all-around nice guy, and I want things to go well. I love that he's all about family first, and I love how he encourages me to be my best."

"That is nice. And I'm sure it doesn't hurt that he has his own business, he's not a ladies man, and he's easy on the eyes."

"Those things are helpful."

"You know what it is, Payton, you finally found yourself a grown man who's not playing around. He's long over the bachelor life, and he's mature. That's the key. Most of us have to wait for our men to grow up. It sounds like you found yourself a ready-made package."

"I definitely feel the difference, but I don't want to get too far ahead of myself. We're just taking it one day at a time."

"Oh, no, you don't."

"What?"

"You're trying to play it safe... 'We're, just taking it one day at a time'." Abby repeated my words.

"You're not fooling me with that baloney, Payton. You've fallen head over heels for this guy. You didn't see it coming, and you just don't want to admit it. Rightfully so. I get it. You've already had one major heartbreak, and you're not looking for another. Just be honest about it because the rest of us can see right through the baloney."

"Oh yeah... Well, You know what?"

Abby placed her hand on her hip and presented a firm stance. "I'm listening."

"You're right," I said, and stopped putting on a facade.

"Okay. You agree with me?"

"Yes, I agree. Not only are you right, but I feel better. I'm not nervous anymore."

"Well, good. Glad to be of service."

"The one thing I can say about the Matthews women is they sure aren't afraid to speak their mind. You being at the top of the list."

"Amen! Wait. What did you just say?"

"I said we are strong women sitting on top of the world."

"I thought I heard something else, but I'm going to let you get away with it this time."

"Hey Ab, I don't want to pry, but I was really concerned about you after that little incident with Susan. How did things turn out?"

"You're not prying. The conversation did take an unexpected turn that day. I spoke to Wyatt after, and he was very straight forward with me. He said the new assistant really did come on strong for a while. He actually had to get HR involved so she would lay off. He was adamant that he went through the proper channels to handle it. He didn't get defensive or anything. He said he just didn't want to upset me with something that was already taken care of. He also called Ross to give him a piece of his mind."

"Wow. That's an awkward position to be in."

"I know you probably have your suspicions, and you're just being gracious not to say anything."

"No, I don't. You know Wyatt better than anyone in this family. If you trust what he's telling you, then so do I. There was a big difference in my situation. Jack was defensive all the time. He would never open up and talk to me. His actions spoke louder than his words."

Abby placed her hand over her heart and then blew a kiss to me.

"Thanks, Sis."

"You're welcome."

"Now, let me go check on the kids before something crashes and breaks."

"Love you, Abby."

"Love you too, Payton."

About three o'clock, Cole arrived with Emmie and his mother. Dad and I greeted them at the door.

"There's my guy. Come on in and make yourself comfortable," Dad said.

"Mr. Matthews, I don't think you've had a chance to meet my mother, Alice Miller, and my daughter Emmie."

"Hello, Mrs. Miller, and hello to the sweet young lady. I'm William Matthews, but my friends call me Will."

"Nice to meet you, Mr. Will." Emmie extended her hand to Dad for a polite handshake.

"Well, don't you have nice manners."

"Yep, that's our Emmie. Don't be fooled by the ten-year-old appearance. She has the maturity of a grown-up."

Emmie smiled proudly at her dad. Then the two of them came over to give me a hug.

Mom joined us in the foyer. "Will, are you going to keep our guests standing in the foyer or let them inside?"

She welcomed everyone into the living room and made instant friends with Cole's mother, Alice.

"You have such a lovely home." Alice looked around.

"Why, thank you. I wish I could take all of the credit, but it belongs to Cole."

"Mrs. Matthews, you can't give me all the credit."

"Oh, Cole, please call me Helen."

"Helen, I just established the framework. You decorated this place to make it feel as cozy as it does. I can't take the credit for that."

"We could go back and forth all day, but I still say that the work you did was the inspiration for everything else."

119

The voice of a little girl rose above the chatter of the adults. "Payton, look what I brought!"

"Ooh, what a beautiful doll. I love her hairstyle."

I could hear Abby talking to Wyatt in the background. "And to think she was nervous earlier."

Emmie's doll was very well put together. I just knew her and my niece Maggie were going to be an instant hit.

"Emmie, I have two very special people that I'd like to introduce you to if you want to come with me."

"Okay."

She followed me over to the two children in the living room who were hiding behind their mother and pretending to be shy.

"Maggie and Aidan, I want you to meet Emmie."

Maggie stepped from behind her mother to say hi to Emmie. Aidan was still on the fence about meeting someone new.

"Emmie, this is my niece Maggie and her brother Aidan who is over there behind his mom."

"Hi, Maggie and Aidan. I brought my American Girl Doll, would you like to play with her?"

"Sure." Maggie tossed caution to the wind and decided to go play.

The girls were about four years apart in age, but Emmie was more of an old soul. She didn't seem to mind taking on the role of a big sister for the day.

"Sorry, Abby. I had every intention of introducing you, but it looks like the girls were able to hit it off right away. Mr. Aidan, on the other hand..."

I tickled my little nephew to pry him loose from his mother.

"What's the shy act all about, bud?"

He looked up at me with the most forgiving smile.

"There's that cute smile. Get on over there and play with your sissy and Emmie."

He took off like a lightning bolt to go show the girls his new sports car.

After all the formal introductions were made, Wyatt cranked up the grill. The guys settled outdoors where they could man the food and watch sports on the big screen while the ladies hung out in the kitchen.

"Payton, I just want you to know that your pictures were a hit with Christen and Jacob. They loved your work so much that Christen has already shared your business card with two other brides. You should be getting calls from them any day now." Alice seemed delighted to share the news.

"That's wonderful. Thank you!"

"You're welcome, but it doesn't stop there. Mrs. Donovan, a long time client of Cole's, was also there the evening of the wedding. She needs someone to do a photoshoot for her website. She owns a boutique in Naples. She said something about needing a few pictures of her latest summer collection."

That name sounded familiar.

"When she saw you at the wedding, she started asking me questions. I made sure I told her about your profession, and the rest, as they say, was history."

"I can't thank you enough. It's my goal to start adding to my client list, and you certainly are helping me get off to a great start."

"It's my pleasure. Stick with me. I know a lot of the ladies down at the church and the social clubs that would love to have you for one event or another."

"Yes, Ma'am. You don't have to tell me twice."

I let the women continue talking while I stepped outside to check on the guys. They were carrying on over their favorite football teams. Dad wouldn't hear of it. He was more of a baseball fan and didn't want anyone stealing his thunder.

"I don't understand how you two are already on to football

talk. For the love of the Gators and all Gators fans, can we save the football talk until at least next month?"

It was fun watching them get all worked up over sports. Of course, being the new guy, Cole gave in.

"Don't let him do it to you, Cole. Stand your ground." Wyatt tried to get Cole back on his side.

"That's what's wrong with the young folks today," Dad said. "You don't have enough of an appreciation for...for... you know. I forgot what I was trying to say, but you know what I mean."

He turned to Cole to further explain.

"Cole, you're going to have to forgive me. Sometimes I'm forgetful."

"Ah, no worries, Sir. You were probably about to get on us for not showing enough love for the Gators."

"That's right."

Wyatt winked at Cole. The family was growing accustomed to the new version of Dad, but it was still an adjustment.

"Alright, we have burgers, hot dogs, and steak. I guess we better get the side fixings. I don't know about you, but I'm ready to eat!" Wyatt was the grandmaster of grilling and usually took on the responsibility whenever he wasn't working.

Later on that evening, we gathered in the living room for a game of charades. Mom pretended to be an astronaut taking small steps for mankind. The others thought she was pretending to be a mummy among a host of other things. Nevertheless, they were still having a good time.

Quite a few times, I laughed so hard I had to go to the bathroom. I saw Cole having just as much fun.

I looked at Cole with a warm smile. "I don't think I'll forget this night for a long time to come."

"That makes two of us. Who knew your mom was such an actress," Cole said.

"Seriously! I sure didn't."

"You know, Payton, I could get use to this."

"Me too... Do you think Emmie and your mom are enjoying themselves?"

"Are you kidding? Mom took great pleasure in beating you in several rounds of Uno. Emmie, on the other hand, has become an instant big sister to your niece and nephew. Just look at her. She's over there pretending to be the teacher and they're her students."

"Ha, you're right. Abby would love to have Emmie around more often. This is the first time in a while the kids haven't tried to tear up the house."

"Would you like to go for a little walk?"

"Sure."

Cole and I excused ourselves from the game to step out back. The wind and the crashing waves were particularly rough as a storm was reported to be heading closer to town.

"Do you hear that?" I asked.

"The sound of the waves?"

"Yes, it's my favorite sound. Growing up as a little girl, that sound used to soothe me until I fell asleep."

"So, you've spent most of your life by the water?"

Cole seemed intrigued by my life story. "I sure have. Until I went to Connecticut, that is. That was really my first experience with living more inland."

"How did you like it?"

"I didn't. Don't get me wrong. Connecticut is a beautiful state. I just wasn't used to the cold winters, and I missed being near the beach."

"They have beaches in Connecticut, don't they?"

"Yes, but it just wasn't the same."

"I can imagine it was the total opposite from what you're accustomed to here in Florida."

"Do you have your sights set on other places to live?" I asked Cole.

"Not really. I think my way of getting to see other places would have to be in the form of going on vacation. With Emmie, Mom, and the business, I can't really see myself picking up and leaving."

"Makes sense. I honestly thought I would never leave. Life has a way of throwing surprises at you."

"True. But now you're back."

"Yes, and hopefully for good. Coming back to Pelican Beach was the best decision I ever made. I didn't realize how much I missed being around the family regularly."

"Can I ask you a candid question?"

"Go for it."

"Do you ever see yourself getting married again someday?"

"To the right one. Not repeating the same mistakes would be my biggest priority."

Cole glanced over at me. He watched as my hair blew in the wind. He watched my lips as I spoke. He slowly turned toward me and pulled me near.

Just then, the sound of the sliding glass door slid open in the background. Emmie stepped outside.

"Dad, Mrs. Matthews wants to know if you and Payton want ice cream?" Emmie said.

We relinquished our embrace.

"Yes, Sweetheart. We're coming right now."

When Emmie left, he slid his finger across my forehead.

"I guess that's our cue."

"Yes, you can't have a family gathering without dessert."

Inside, mom prepared a buffet of toppings and different flavored ice cream for everyone to enjoy.

"Everybody, dig in. There's plenty to go around."

"Helen, you are spoiling us. We're going to have to walk all of this off later," Cole said as he made his way around the table.

"Oh, anything for the Millers. We're so happy you're here." She gave Cole a wink and smiled at me. I think it was safe to assume that she thought Cole was a keeper.

"Mom, where's Rebecca?"

"She said something about not wanting to be here without a date. I think she chose to bury herself in work instead."

"What? That's crazy."

"You know your sister. When she gets stuck on something, she has a hard time letting it go. In her mind, everyone coming today would be with their special someone. I don't know, Payton. Sometimes it's hard to get through to her."

Alice tried to offer words of comfort.

"I'm flying solo and having a great time. Someone should've called and encouraged her to come over."

"I told her it wasn't for couples only, but what can you do?"

"I don't know her story, but it's not easy being alone. Frank's been gone for over eight years now, and I still miss him like crazy."

"That makes two of us," Cole said.

"I'm sorry, Alice."

"Thank you, Helen. Obviously I'm blessed to have Cole and Emmie to look after me. But when I'm by myself for too long, it can be a little difficult. Taking care of Emmie gives me something to look forward to."

"That certainly makes sense. I believe Rebecca will meet the right one someday. She just has to stop comparing herself to her sisters and stop being so hard on herself. Not everyone is on the same time table."

I let the mothers continue to talk while I joined the kids in the living room. Emmie was reading a book to Maggie and

Aidan. I waited until she finished before striking up a conversation. "Emmie, you are an amazing reader."

"Thank you. My teacher always tells me to read lots and lots of books. She says that books take you on adventures."

"You're teacher sounds pretty smart. What kind of adventure were you reading about today?"

"Oh, we were just reading Maggie's book about the Magic Treehouse. Have you heard of the Magic Treehouse before?"

"Have I heard of the Magic Treehouse? Those books are amazing."

"Do you have kids?"

"No, I don't have kids of my own, but I spend quite a bit of time with these two little rascals." Emmie giggled as I playfully poked them in the tummy.

"Payton, do you know what I think?" I stopped to listen.

"I think we should all plan a beach day!" Then she turned to everyone and said, "If you like to build sandcastles, raise your hand."

Everyone raised their hands, including Cole, who came and sat on the floor with the crew.

"Emmie Miller, I would be very shocked if you didn't become a teacher someday. You're always asking everyone to raise their hands like they're in class." Cole laughed.

"Aww, that's sweet, Emmie. I love to build sandcastles. And if you ever did become a teacher, I think all the children in Pelican Beach would love to be in your class!"

She did have a way with leading the group. I thought it was rather cute.

As the evening came to an end, I walked the Millers out to their car. It sounds kind of silly, but I was sad to see them go.

Alice reached out to give me a hug. "Payton, thank you again for such a lovely evening. I felt right at home with your family."

"Aww, Alice, that makes my heart happy. Get ready because the Matthews are known for their parties."

"I'll be there with bells on. You tell Rebecca we're sorry she didn't come, and we can't wait to meet her next time."

"I will."

Alice got in the car to give us a moment to say goodbye. Emmie squeezed my waist and then hopped in the back seat.

"Bye, Payton."

"I'll see you, Emmie."

I turned to Cole to say my goodbyes. "Cole, send me a quick message to let me know you guys make it home okay."

"I'll do one better. How about I send you a text, and then once I get the little one to bed, I'll give you a call to plan our next date?"

"I like the way you think. I'll be waiting."

"Sounds good." He gave me a kiss on the cheek before getting in the car and leaving. And now for the difficult part... to make it back into the house without squealing out loud!

PAYTON

O n Monday, we hosted a brunch at the Inn to say our
final farewells to the staff. We were stunned to see the
outpouring of gifts to wish my parents a happy retirement.

Shelby was first in line to wish them well.

"Mr. and Mrs. Matthews, what are we going to do without
you?"

"Aww, Shelby, we feel the same way about all of you. This
place has been our livelihood, and we wouldn't have made it
without wonderful staff members such as yourself. Thank you
for always greeting our guests and taking good care of them."

Once everyone had an opportunity to dine and mingle,
Mom tapped her glass to make a speech.

"Ladies and gentlemen, may I have your attention."

She motioned for Dad to join her.

"It has been such an honor to work side by side with you as
we served the guests of the Inn over the years. As many of you
are aware, William and I have decided to retire. It's a bittersweet time for us, but just like the seasons of life don't last
forever, we knew our time here wouldn't last forever. All of us

have spent some of the best times of our lives here together. We've watched some of you get married, have children, and you've even watched us as we raised children of our own. Through it all, we've been a family."

She then turned to Dad and asked if he'd like to say a few words.

"I don't know that I can add much more to what Helen has said. She always puts her words together so eloquently. But please know from the bottom of our hearts..."

Dad choked up and started to cry as he stood before everyone.

"Please know that although we will no longer be here at the Inn with you, we will truly miss you. We can't thank you enough for your years of service and support. We wish you all the best."

Not an eye in the room was dry. Helen then held up her glass and said, "To great health and many blessings upon your future endeavors. Cheers!"

"Cheers." The staff clapped and celebrated the end of a lovely era with the Matthews family. I took several pictures to create an album as a keepsake for my parents. Tomorrow would be a difficult day as they would hand the keys over at closing, but for now, my parents made the most of their last few hours as owners of the Inn.

Later that evening, once everyone was settled back at home, I accepted an invitation from Cole for a quiet date for two at his place. Emmie was at her grandmother's for the weekend.

"Cole, seriously? Are you really covering my eyes with blindfolds?"

I stood with my car keys in hand, smiling in disbelief. This guy was always up to something. I can't lie, I loved it.

"Yes, I am. I'm sorry, but you can't be trusted. And since I worked very hard on this surprise, I don't want you to ruin it."

He stood back and looked at my sundress before carrying on with his charade.

"Come on, Pay. Be a good sport."

"Alright, alright."

He tied the blindfold from behind and led me toward the house.

"Okay, we're going around back like we did last time. Follow me."

"Haha, that's funny. I don't have any other choice."

Instead of stopping at the back of his house, it felt like we were going closer to the water.

"We seem to be going further than I remembered."

"You're pretty good. That's because we are going a bit further. I'm going to stop for a minute because I need you to give me your sandals."

"My sandals? Cole Miller, what are you up to?"

"You trust me, don't you?"

I sighed and lifted up one foot at a time as not to be difficult.

"You know I don't like surprises."

"I beg to differ. I think you love surprises, you just want to know what it is right away."

"You might have a good point there."

"We're making our way on to the sand and then just a few more steps, and we're there."

The excitement was building up. I held his hand so tight, not knowing what to expect.

"Let me get the blindfold for you. Should we do a count down or..."

"I can't take it anymore."

He removed the blindfold. A beautiful table was set before me. It was covered in white linen with candles that were lit for a centerpiece. White Christmas tree lights surrounded the trim of his deck and led all the way down to our table on the beach. It was a romantic dinner for two.

"Oh... my... gosh. Cole, this is amazing. How in the world?"

"I had to get a little creative. Do you like it?"

"Do I like it? I love it! How special is this? And the lights trailing all the way from the house. I'm speechless."

"You deserve it. When is the last time someone went out of their way to express their love for you?"

Did he just say his love for me?

He pulled out a chair for me to sit. There were stainless steel dish covers over our plates and a bucket of wine.

"Unbelievable. I thought we might throw a couple of burgers on the grill, but you really outdid yourself."

"Only the best for you, Miss Matthews. Only the best."

"You better be careful with how much you spoil me. A girl could get used to this kind of treatment."

"I wouldn't do anything for you now that I don't plan on doing for the rest of my life."

"Well, clearly, you can see that I can't stop smiling, so thank you. This means a lot to me."

"Hold that thought. I want to pick up on what you just said in a minute, but I also don't want your food to get cold. Now, before I uncover the plates, I want you to promise not to laugh at me."

"I promise."

Lifting the covers from the plates he exposed a burger and fries from my favorite restaurant.

"No wayyyy." I laughed so hard. I couldn't help it. Thankfully Cole lost it and laughed too.

"Hey, you promised."

"I know, I know... I'm not laughing at you!"

"Let me guess. You're laughing with me?"

"Something like it."

"Hey, for me, this is fine cuisine." He teased.

"It's mighty fine, alright. You almost had me fooled with the bottled wine and the stainless steel covers."

"I know. It's kind of pathetic, I would have to agree. Now you know something else about me. I can't cook to save my life."

"What? How do you feed Emmie?"

"Luckily, Emmie is pretty easy going. She's used to my cooking. If I ever make something that's too horrible, then we opt for take out. I didn't want to subject you to my home-cooked meals just yet."

"Aww, Cole. I think this is so cute and so thoughtful. Everything is wonderful. Even down to the burgers."

"Are you sure?"

"Yes, and I'm sorry for laughing. I just couldn't help it."

"That's okay, I thought it was funny myself. As I was standing at the counter waiting for the food, I was thinking, 'man, you really need some cooking lessons'."

"Well, there's an idea. We should take lessons. All three of us. I'm sure Emmie would love it, and I could always stand to pick up a pointer or two."

"Emmie would love that."

In between eating fries, our feet brushed together under the table. There was definitely chemistry between us that couldn't be denied.

"To pick up where we left off. It means a lot to me that you're here, sharing this moment with me. I remember the first time we met in the lobby at the Inn. I had no clue when I woke up that day that I would meet the woman who would later capture my heart."

"Neither did I. You were so into your measurements; I don't know how you had time to even notice me."

"Oh, I noticed you! By the time I was making my way back to your dad's office, I was thinking, wow. I don't know what it was. You had a little spice in you as you stood there with your arms folded, and you looked absolutely beautiful. I know you were probably standing there thinking, 'what's this fool doing in the lobby'?"

"Perhaps. But Mom set me straight really quick."

"She did?"

"Yep. She started going on and on about how you are one of the most respected renovators in town, and how you worked on the cottage. I'm just sorry you never had a chance to do the project at the Inn. I'm sure you would've really made that place look spectacular."

"You know, Payton. In hindsight, I wasn't sent there for the job."

"What do you mean?"

"I was probably sent there just to meet you."

I thought that was such a sweet thing to say. If this was a dream, I felt like someone needed to wake me up soon before I fell in too deep.

"Do you know what would be the perfect addition to this evening?"

"I honestly don't know. The night is already perfect from where I sit."

"I have one more teeny tiny surprise. It's nothing big. Just a small added touch to make the evening extra special."

"Uh, oh."

"No, uh oh's. I promise. Come here."

He held his hand out to invite me to dance.

"I can handle this kind of surprise, but there's no music. What are we dancing to?"

Cole gently pulled me closer.

"Close your eyes."

At the click of a button, the music began to serenade us on his CD player.

"You seemed to like the idea of a private dance party, so I thought I could arrange one for you."

We swayed to the music and sang the lyrics together.

"I can't sing very well, but I can kiss you under the light of a thousand stars." I gladly accepted his invitation.

"I thought you would never ask."

Placing his lips softly on mine, I returned a passionate kiss.

For me, love was taking on a whole new meaning. Love brought me into this world, raised me as a little child, and nurtured me as a woman. But love didn't always come with its highs. Sometimes it brought tears and heartache. Thankfully, this time, love was giving me a second chance.

ALSO BY MICHELE GILCREST

Sunsets At Pelican Beach- Pelican Beach Series Book 2

Ready to read Book 2 in the Pelican Beach series?

Moving on from her divorce and finding love again was the best thing that happened to Payton in a long time. After all, who could resist the charm of the handsome and well respected Cole Miller?

Unfortunately all it takes is one bad apple to spoil everything...

In book two of the Pelican Beach series Payton's new photography client proves that she can't be trusted around Cole. Have you ever met someone who's willing to do whatever it takes to have their way? Well, that describes the new competition, Lexi Donovan. Will Payton stand by her man and protect what's hers or will she get fed up and walk away?

In the midst of Payton balancing her love life there's a family scare that sends everyone into a panic. The family would be absolutely devastated if the scare were to end in tragedy.

Then there's the three sisters... will Payton and her sisters thrive through all of the family drama or barely survive? Some unexpected news will push their relationship to the test!

Pack your bags and enjoy beautiful sunsets at Pelican Beach! Just like anywhere you may visit there will be a little drama, and maybe even some unwanted competition. But the main dish being served in this book is sweet love!

Also By Michele Gilcrest

Pelican Beach Series

The Inn At Pelican Beach: Book 1

Sunsets At Pelican Beach: Book 2

A Pelican Beach Affair: Book 3

Christmas At Pelican Beach: Book 4

Cortland Series

Second Time Around: Book 1

Tried and True : Book 2

CPSIA information can be obtained
at www.ICGtesting.com
Printed in the USA
LVHW021327230121
677173LV00005B/497